Cassandra's Comet

By Cameron Glenn

Smashwords Edition

Copyright 2016 Cameron Glenn

This book is licensed for your personal enjoyment only. This book may not be re-sold or given away to other people. If you would like to share this book with another person, please purchase an additional copy for each recipient. If you're reading this book and did not purchase it, or it was not purchased for your use only, then please return to Smashwords.com or your favorite retailer and purchase your own copy. Thank you for respecting the hard work of this author.

CASSANDRA'S COMET

*

CHAPTER ONE

A painted map of the United States laid on the black concrete next to the four square lines on the playground of Jefferson Grade School in Salt Lake City. Cassandra, age nine, took a gentle step over Florida and then another step and she stood over Georgia. She looked down and watched a white moth flutter and land on her neon red shoelaces. She took a hop and the moth flew off and she landed in Nashville; another hop and spin took her near Cleveland, standing near the Great Lakes above Michigan. With each step, in her mind she heard bomb explosions; the sounds she overheard from the television when her father watched World War II documentaries on the History Channel. She unconsciously mimicked this bomb sound with her mouth as she stepped, tightening her lips, letting air build up in her cheeks, then releasing the craggily noise in a burst which scratched the back of her throat and then dissipated into a blow: *Bkhuuu... Bkhuuu...*

The white noise of her peers circled around her: the laughing and squealing of dodging and chasing; Hands grabbing and swinging from monkey bars showing off new skills and tricks; A contest of who could swing the highest on the swings in the sawdust, leaping off daringly and dangerously to see who is most brave and crazy; Clumps of kids rushing at scooting soccer balls in the grass field beyond; all 'kids at play' noises which were drowned out by the sounds of the bombs falling from clouds creating the destruction of everything which played out in Cassandra's mind. *Bkhuuu... Bkhuuu...*

She heard the voice of a man tell her: *It will happen in the desert.* She couldn't tell if the voice belonged to the Light Man or the Shadow Man. Their voices often sounded indistinguishable. "I know" she answered the voice.

She hop-skipped towards the four corners region where the borders of Arizona, Colorado, Utah and New Mexico collide.

"What are you doing?" she heard a voice outside her head ask in a judgmental accusatory tone.

She looked up and saw Jeremy sneering at her.

"It will hit the United States first," Cassandra said.

"What will?" Jeremy asked.

"The comet. My comet."

"You're a freak," Jeremy scoffed.

"I know what your stepfather does to your sister Jeremy," Cassandra said in a near whisper. Her chin bowed near her neck and she looked up at him with her large aqua-grey eyes through her dark dirty blonde bangs.

Jeremy balled his right hand into a fist and narrowed his eyes. Through tight lips he said: "I don't know what you're talking about."

"You do know," Cassandra shot back in her low measured tone. "You've seen her bruises. You ignore the truth because you don't want it to be real. You're afraid. You allow her to suffer."

"You freak!" Jeremy yelled in a rage. He raised his fist and lunged hard towards Cassandra's jaw. An invisible force held his fist. He could not move it. He thought of the class experiment on magnets from last week. He wiggled his arm but his fists were stuck in place, glued in mid-air. His gasp became a groan as the force pushed in on his knuckles. He looked at Cassandra. She stood firm, motionless. She walked closer to him, like examining an ice statue. His face had never been so close to a girl before. Even in his rage, confusion and panic, the first time thought also struck him: Cassandra is pretty. She had light freckles across the bridge of her nose and cheeks. He hadn't looked beyond her class freak moniker to ever consider her anything beyond what she was ridiculed as: the class freak quiet girl everyone tried to ignore. He panted another breathy groan and again unsuccessfully tried to wiggle his fist free. "You... freak," he whispered.

"Tell me Jeremy? Is the world worth saving?" Cassandra sounded sincere in her question.

"I..." Jeremy stammered.

Cassandra put her soft face even closer to his. He was sweating. He squirmed, still stuck. "Kiss me," she said her lips close to his ear. "Show me the world is worth saving or not."

Jeremy again struggled to move but was as helpless as when his older brother pinned him down, threatening to drop a strand of saliva on his face. He grunted a high pitched squeal from frustration. "Let me go!" he screamed. Right after his scream the pressure on his hand released. He fell limp onto the black concrete. He scraped his knee. He got up, shaky legged and brushed little rocks off his knees and hands. He couldn't look at her in her eyes. He wanted to scream at her and threaten her and run off and report her and get her into trouble. But to yell at her he'd have to look at her in the eyes. And he found that he could not do that. He feared her. He feared his confusion over her power. He massaged his previously fisted hand. His shaky legs gave out and he plopped back down, his rump on the hard black concrete. He whimpered worryingly while looking at his slightly swollen numbed hand as he tried to flex his fingers. His whimper became a silent sob as he realized he were in the act of peeing himself, the sudden warm then sudden cold yellow liquid becoming a puddle around him, his pants around his crotch area soaked through. He cried from embarrassment and failure.

Cassandra turned her back to him. She took another step placing her foot over the four corners area where Utah, New Mexico, Colorado and Arizona converge. *Bkhuuu...*

CHAPTER TWO

"I try not to speak," Cassandra mumbled. "When I do I get in trouble."

"Please, feel free to speak; no need to be nervous, I won't bite," the principle said through a strained and forced awkward grin.

Cassandra sat in a large wood chair, her hands in her lap, fingers clasped, her feet dangling. She faced the school principle who sat behind his large mahogany desk decorated with a red wax apple and a small glass bowl of jolly ranchers set at opposite corners. His elbows rested on the desktop, his hands clasped with his pointer fingers extended, resting over his small lips. He peered down at her through his glasses resting on the tip of his nose. As usually happens whenever Cassandra sat in front of him, he found himself engaged in something of an impromptu staring contest with her while his thoughts meandered to wondering why she didn't blink, especially with her eyes so big. He stiffened his back and cleared his throat, struggling to not allow her frozen glassy eyes to unsettle or distract him. Her stiffness, seriousness, strangeness, all left him with the discomforting impression that this cute little girl held some type of power or authority over him; the reverse of how it should be. *He* should be making *her* feel uncomfortable, not visa-versa.

He looked into her eyes. They pulled him in. He could not look away. What color are they, he wondered: blue, green, grey; are those gold flecks in them? How is it that they appear to glow and that the color in her eyes seems to swirl like they were made of vibrating amebas? The more his thoughts wondered on her eyes, the deeper her eyes sucked him in, causing him to break through their glassy surface, to swim through them. The metaphysical sensations became physical so that the being pulled forward sensation felt actual, like a soul tripping free from the hold of a body. He blinked. When his eyes opened he found himself floating through a black honey like substance. He couldn't breathe. But he didn't need to breathe. He wondered if he had died. He noticed a star faintly twinkling below him, then another above him. The stars increased in brightness and others began to poke through the blackness. Then gold and blue swirling galaxies emerged, populating the space around him, illuminating beautifully. The expansive beauty of the surrounding stars and galaxies both terrified and awed him. He began to shake. He heard and felt a rumbling, which increased, vibrating his insides as if his head lay on a metal rail while a locomotive thundered towards him.

He gasped, deeply inhaling while throwing his head back as one does when in emergency need of air, breaking free of submergence, or suddenly jolting awake from a moment of peril within a nightmare. He found himself sitting back in his chair behind his desk again. His heart raced. He felt as if he should be wet although he was dry. He glanced at the clock on the wall, then the watch on his wrist. No time had passed at all despite feeling as if he had been trapped within Cassandra's eyes for minuets. He sensed her large eyes still barreling into him, through him, through his essence, his thoughts, his memories, his past and even his future. He vowed never to become trapped and lulled into looking at her eyes again. He spread his fingers across his desk fumbling for invisible papers to shuffle, as a stall tactic in order to try and regain himself. He cleared his throat.

"You felt it, didn't you?" Cassandra asked.

"Felt what?"

"A spec of what I feel. The force of it. Hurling towards us."

The principle gurgled something inaudible.

"I know you," Cassandra said. "I know what you look at on your computer."

Sweat trickled down from the principle's sideburn.

"The comets fire will cleanse your soul," Cassandra said, in an eerie slightly higher register, a tinge of compassion in her tone.

"Cassandra," the principle said with his head down, avoiding her eyes. He then sensed her jerk her head violently to the side, like the head of a bird swiveling towards an insect which just zipped by. Her movement was so unexpected and quick that it caused him to jolt also; his knee involuntarily kicked the underside of his desk, causing a loud bang. Cassandra's head darted in the other direction with the hyper quick and inhuman reflex of a agitated bird on lookout perched on a branch.

"Do you hear something? What is it?" the principle asked.

Cassandra centered her head and stared directly at the principle again, unblinking. He darted his eyes away from hers. *Compose yourself,* he thought. He cleared his throat.

"Cassandra, are you familiar with the term, sexual discrimination?" he asked, placing his elbows back on his desk, learning forward, looking down at his interlocked fingers. *What a strange thing I just asked a nine year old girl* he thought. *But she's not in any way like a normal nine year old girl. She's strange.*

"Is sexual harassment the way you think of Mrs. Mullins when you imagine her bending over weeding her tomatoes naked?" Cassandra asked more as an accusation than a question.

After a pause from shock the principle coughed and then cleared his throat, deciding it best to simply ignore her quip as if she hadn't said it, similar to how one who first sees a ghost in peripheral vision decides to dismiss and ignore it, thinking it cannot be. He shifted in his seat, trying to ignore another cool drop of sweat burning his temples. "Jeremy claims that you... threatened to kill...I mean kiss... or kill him unless he... that if he didn't that you'd..." the principle stammered.

"I said no such thing."

The principle cleared his throat again, stiffened his back and forced himself to try and glance at her eyes again, careful not to look beyond their glassy surface, determined to dismiss the spell her eyes had earlier entrapped him in, or to feel intimidated or frightened by a little girl. He internally scolded himself: *She is a child in my authority; it is my responsibility to ensure and enforce the comfort and safety of the school cultural environment as a whole; to make it conductive to learning and positive development... she is so strange... and no, Mrs. Smarty pants, solitary sexual fantasies do not immediately constitute sexual harassment...* He snapped back into focus before his thoughts unraveled further.

"Cassandra," he said, trying to sound authoritative. He realized after he had said her name that he didn't know what to say next, how to scold her, what to charge her with or reprimand her for. He cleared his throat again; his constant throat clearing when uncomfortable a habit he knew others found annoying but he could not stop any easier than refusing to scratch an itchy nose. He decided to change his tone from hard to soft, poor girl, it must be difficult to be so strange and isolated, after all. He relaxed his stiffness and slumped forwards. "Are things all right at home?" he asked, trying to sound tender. "You come from a single father household right? No siblings... does he..."

"Don't worry Principle Holebrook, I won't be here for long."

"I... you're moving?" He felt only slightly guilty that the thought of her moving was a relief.

"It's my tenth birthday in a few days."

"Yes...I... happy birthday," he answered perplexed.

"In my tenth year in 2010 is when it will happen," Cassandra declared.

"What will happen?"

"I watched the alpenglow on the mountains last night," she said. "During the sunset."

The principle stared at her blankly, still careful to avoid locking into her pretty eyes.

"Alpenglow means the colors of the setting sun reflecting off the mountains of the opposite horizon," Cassandra said as if reciting a memorized dictionary definition. "The Light Man told me that," she added.

"The... who?"

"The mountains were covered in snow," Cassandra said. "And they turned pink and purple, the shadows in the mountain crevices blue. And I turned around and saw the sun setting at the other horizon, lighting the underbellies of the scattered grey snow clouds aflame. The 'V' pattern of Canadian Geese flew above me."

"That's... nice," the principle answered with uncertainty, wondering why she'd say such a thing to him, (how strange she talked, even if she were a grown up) what might it mean. He wanted her to leave; he still tried to dismiss his discomfort with her as if trying to ignore a large centipede crawling up his arm. The seconds felt heavy. He still sweat from her comment about Mrs. Mullins (the new teacher fresh from college) gardening naked. How had she known?

"Last time it rained the Shadow Man made the rain look like blood," Cassandra declared. "I didn't know if it was real or one of his visions at first. I saw it falling from the sky to splat and smear the window. The smell of blood overpowered me. It smells like salty rusted metal. And death. Rot. The body rots so quickly after the soul leaves. Rancid flesh, food for larva, empty containers, garbage; we're all eventual garbage, the Shadow Man told me, and to clean garbage you burn it, to purify and sweep it away, ashes to the sky, to do away with all our evil inside us." As Cassandra made her speech she rose to her feet, her voice becoming a crescendo of crashing waves from the dull drizzle it had started out as. "And I stepped out in the blood and it covered me and I cried and the blood caught on fire as if gasoline, and fire fell from the sky..."

"Enough!" the principle burst out, interrupting her, chasing away his fear with a defiant scream. "That is enough Cassandra!"

Cassandra closed her mouth, bowed her head and demurely sat back in the large wood chair facing the principle. "He shows me such horrible things," she mumbled in a whisper.

"What?" the principle asked.

"Nothing. When I speak I get into trouble. I try not to speak," Cassandra answered.

The principle cleared his throat.

"The Light Man shows me beauty. In nature and people. At least he tries. He says people are good and the world is worth saving. That I should let my comet pass over it as harmlessly as a sparkler bursting and fading against the night on the Fourth of July. The Dark Man shows me ugly things. Genocides. Holocaust. Hate. The screams of victims. No one is guiltless. Have you seen a holocaust Principle Holbrook?"

Most girls your age collect pink rubber ponies and silly bandz bracelets and sleep hugging stuffed animals and obsess over Justin Bieber, the principle thought. *How can you speak like you do? It's unnatural to the point of unholiness. Why do you always look so sad and heavy despite being so thin and frail? Why does looking at you make me feel so heavy? So strange?*

"I...no, not personally," the principle answered. Then he heard Cassandra's voice loud and clear in his mind say so pointedly it felt like a needle pricked his ear: *you will.* He almost scolded her for threatening him and considered calling the police or social services to have her detained and evaluated as a threat or a terrorist or a menace, but then he realized that her mouth hadn't moved when he heard her voice. He then wondered if maybe she weren't the crazy one but he was. He hated her for making him question his sanity. For making him consider calling the police to have a nine year old girl (almost ten) arrested simply for creeping him out. Although, there have been a few cases, rare yet reported, of nine year olds murdering and setting trailer homes and schools on fire. He made a mental note to call Cassandra's father to persuade him to take her to a psychologist to have her evaluated, diagnosed, and helped (hopefully taken out of school) for clearly *something* disturbed this cute, large eyed, malnourished yet heavy looking, magical or wicked strange little girl.

"Candy?" the principle asked and scooted the glass bowl of jolly ranchers across the desk towards her. Cassandra leapt off her chair and plunged her hand into the candy bowl and pulled out a handful. The principle forced a smile. Cassandra forced a smile back.

"Don't worry principle Holebrook, I won't tell anyone about you and Mrs. Mullins," Cassandra said.

The principle fought his urge to become defensive and mock offense in retorting that he had no idea what she were talking about, in a thinly veiled attempt to persuade her of his innocence. Instead he again forced a smile at her. "Go back to class," he instructed. "Don't threaten to kiss any more boys. ...Or talk about weird things."

"I'll die before I kiss anyone," Cassandra breathily mumbled forlornly, looking at the floor as she stuffed the jolly ranchers in her pockets.

"I hope you won't be leaving us. We'd miss you," he lied.

"You shouldn't lie," Cassandra mumbled inaudibly.

"What's that? Remember; don't be afraid to speak up."

"I shouldn't speak," Cassandra said. She then turned and walked towards the door with her hands clasped behind her back. The principle slumped, frowned and wiped his damp forehead with his sleeve.

CHAPTER THREE

*

Jasper currently lived in Atlanta but in his sixteen years his father had dragged him to seven different states and enrolled him in nine different schools and he knew he'd move again soon. One of the perks of being the only son of a single father who led a small nomadic cult in search of some supposed "prophet girl" is that you get to see a lot of the country.

The first stipulation his father would make of these temporary abodes in these new neighborhoods he'd replant to, is that they contain basements; the creepier and more run down the better, seemed to be the criteria. The cult, a group of about only twenty who called themselves *The Blue Magenie Family,* five of whom considered themselves psychics, would decorate these basements with blue silk drapes and long white candles on medieval looking long iron candle holders. Then they'd fill the room with various paintings and drawings, (some good in realist style, done with care and craft, others abstract, done quick and hastily while in some type of vigorous hallucinatory trance) that the psychics had created, all images of this little girl, this lost yet living prophet said to have been born around the year 2000, who was the object of their worship. They believed that it was their clans destiny to find this girl and save her so that she could rescue the world from the fourth apocalypse (according to this cult's doctrine there had been three prior earth apocalypses, or 'mass extinction events', one of which killed off the dinosaurs). Strangely, or perhaps not so strangely, the psychics artistic interpretations of the girl all varied, except that she was young and had large eyes; a common motif was to display stars in her pupils; some symbolic meaning, Jasper concluded, which was beyond his understanding (not that he put much effort in trying to understand, to the dismay of his father).

At around age twelve, only four years ago but seemingly a lifetime ago, in that way years contain greater separation to the rapidly developing young than they do the stagnant and decaying adult, he had decided to stop trying to understand, or even necessarily believe in, all the tenants and ways of his father's cult, despite, admittedly, seeing some strange unexplainable things during ceremonies and trances and experiencing some occasions of what could be called spiritual manifestations. His father, to his credit, Jasper thought, didn't force him to go to the services or ceremonies or to believe in the religion, although he admitted to being severely disappointed. *Whether you believe or not,* his father had told him, *you will be instrumental. It has been foretold.*

Back when Jasper still talked to his father about the religion he had asked him if there were any others in the world like them; how strange it is that if we are the holders of this truth concerning the end of the world, and this girl who will save it, that we'd be the only ones who know. His father reminded him of *The Red Mangenie Family;* they too know of the prophet girl and the end times, although their philosophy is different. Their desire is not to save the young prophet but to kill her so that she cannot save the world. They consider saving the world to be impeding with nature. The extinction of the dinosaurs had caused the environment which enabled mankind to come into being and to evolve, yet over the last centuries mankind has become rotten. They believe that the human tree must be pruned in order for a new branch to grow, for new hope to emerge, for they believe that there is no hope; that we have already failed. *That almost makes sense,* Jasper had thought, thinking of all the wars, hatreds, racism, terrorism and other evils of humans in recent history. 'Make no mistake, they are evil,' his father had then admonished. 'They'd have billions of lives, all of humanity, destroyed, wiped away. We can't let that happen. We must prevail. They are our enemies, going back generations; you remember our history, right son? The great split of 1580? The Blue Mangine's psychics are disrupting our own, making it difficult to pinpoint just where our rescuer resides. Meanwhile our own psychics have to waste time clouding their psychic's images so that they do not find the prophet in order to destroy her.' It was at that point that Jasper felt like rolling his eyes. It all just sounded too silly. He figured he had just been born with a 'doubting Thomas' seed in him.

Jasper laid on the ragged couch, freshly showered, watching the Spurs-Knicks game on mute, his earphones on, listening to an indie-rock song a cute girl in his class liked. He had just finished *Batman Arkham Asylum* on his PS3 about an hour ago. A half hour or so ago he had clicked around on the computer and had come across a video of a French girl stripping. With his father occupied down in the basement, engaged in his cult business, he knew he could get away with watching the video. Maybe the girl wasn't French but she danced to a French song and had brown hair pulled up in a high pony tail, was skinny and energetic, had soft smooth creamy skin and svelte shoulders. *Where did she come from? What is this?* He had heard a bump hit the floor from below and he quickly closed the video.

He liked to keep himself distracted and overly stimulated on the nights of his father's cult basement meetings. He didn't want to think about whatever weird stuff went on down there: chanting, conjuring spirits, blood drawings (the psychics would sometimes prick their fingers and draw images with their blood on each other's faces and on paper while the other cult members chanted ancient verses) or who knows what all else; he only came to more fully realize the strangeness of these rituals and meetings at around age ten when he began to ask his school friends about their own religious beliefs and meetings. His father had instructed him to keep the cult a secret; if anyone asks tell them you're Christian, which Jasper had always done. He had found it strange, when talking with classmates, that animal spirits didn't show up and run around during their own church services, and when his questions, such as *you've never seen a burning hand before?* Were met with blank stares and ridiculing guffaws, he quickly learned to avoid the topic of religion. Which became easy since he never stayed in any one place long enough to develop the type of bonds which cultivate deep discussions. After the fourth move he had stopped making an effort to make new friends anyways, knowing he'd soon have to leave them.

Ginoblie of the Spurs banked in a wild left handed layup, a circus shot, and Jasper imagined the impassioned shout of Charles Barkley yell out "Ginoblie!" *Never met another girl like you,* the "Smith Westerns" singer breezily sung as a love struck sigh into Jasper's ear. Another song started, his iPhone music playlist on shuffle; another sappy love song by an earnest indie-rock band, yet with a bit of fuzz in the guitars. Then, Spurs up two, five minutes left, "Girl Inform Me," by the Shins played. He wanted the Spurs to lose.

Jasper thought of girls. *Where had that French girl gotten those candy striped white pants? Just how far did she go? Is it just dumb luck dad hasn't caught me yet?* He was sixteen and had never been kissed. Just that afternoon he had a jolting encounter with a petite girl named Lucy who had recently lost her virginity (so the rumors went) and cut her hair; a pretty girl who he had a half crush on since he had half crushes on nearly every pretty girl he saw. She had stomped up to him during lunch wearing a tight peach t-shirt as he sat alone at a table. She pounded her hands near his lunch tray and leaned over him causing her imitation gold heart necklace to dangle limp in front of her slung cleavage, which Jasper gaped at then looked away in embarrassment and befuddlement as he sucked chocolate milk up from his straw.

"Just what is your problem!" she had scolded.

"Um... excuse me?" Jasper had hesitantly replied.

"I know you like me. You think I haven't noticed you staring at me?"

Jasper had then blushed and looked away while sipping the last remnants of the chocolate milk, inhaling air in his search for more, causing the dry slurping sucking sound which added to the awkwardness. "Don't flatter yourself," he then mumbled without looking at her.

"Really?" Lucy had then retorted, raising her eyebrows, shifting her shoulder at him, learning forwards and closer, knowingly exposing more cleavage.

Jasper had then wondered *why do you care,* except that he knew the answer: girls often found him attractive; a predicament which embarrassed him more than emboldened him. He had natural muscular build without having to exercise much, and soft grey eyes, another genetic blessing. Sometimes when fresh out of the shower he'd slick his hair back and flex his biceps while practicing his smolder pose, only half jokingly thinking that he could pass as a Calvin Kline model.

Perhaps his perceived aloofness, taking the loner route, offended the egos of some of these girls which somehow made him more desirable to them, he mused. He tried to recall exactly what he had said to Lucy after she confronted him: something along the lines of, *I move around a lot, I've learned not to get attached; I wouldn't want to break your heart.* But, he recalled, while he had said this his thoughts had been something along the lines of: *my gosh, you're so sexy, a little slutty, but cool seeming; you look cute with that new haircut, what was sex like, is that rumor true; are you emotionally vulnerable now; wow, your breasts are perfect; why am I so shy, so stupid, so afraid; is it because I'm embarrassed by my father and his cult?*

But of course she couldn't answer his thoughts, only his arrogant seeming words which she had retorted with: "It's not my heart I want you to touch." Wow. Jasper couldn't handle that flirty repartee, not suave or clever or confident enough, so instead he just looked away, blushed harder, fumbled with his tray and got up and left while he imagined Lucy shaking her head in dismay and disgust at him, this *scared little boy;* any attraction she previously held for him vanished, for the allure of confidence is stronger to a girl than even looks, and the lack of confidence as repellant, or more so, than bad body odor.

The Spurs game ended, the Lakers-Nuggets game started. *What's the matter with me* Jasper wondered while still lying on the couch.

He wasn't gay. He knew that. He'd love to date and make out with girls; he could if he wanted to; Lucy, yes, but there were others like her at other schools; why didn't he? Shyness played a part but that wasn't all of it. Perhaps fear of letting a girl get close to him to then be freaked out by his dad and run away in horror; embarrassment from that prospect wouldn't let him get close to a girl and maybe he was just the type of guy who couldn't or didn't want to kiss and feel and slobber all over a girl without developing a emotional closeness to her as well, which would require her to learn about his father and the crazy cult, Jasper mused. *Maybe I'm just too much a damn gentleman.* Or maybe this end-of-the-world doomsday doctrine poured so thick into his subconscious that he couldn't help but subconsciously feel that everything is futile, so no use in trying for anything, including obtaining a girlfriend; however, he continued to wonder, if I really did believe the earth were ending soon, in my subconscious or whatever, if the cult fails in its mission to rescue the little prophet girl or whatever, and the other red cult wins, then wouldn't I try to live free from fear of consequences and be more reckless, daring, and selfish, since everything will end anyways? Who knows.

Kobe Bryant hit a three followed by a Ron Artest three pointer and Jasper turned the channel; he hated the Lakers and didn't want to watch them win.

While flipping channels he delved deeper into his lazy psychological self-analysis, wondering why an adequate looking guy, at least, like him had never kissed a girl, thus making him one of the biggest losers on earth. There was a deeper, perhaps more accurate reason he knew, which he had been denying and dismissing because of its strangeness. He may have already fallen in love with a girl who doesn't exist.

This girl manifest herself from an experience during a cult ceremony. The old lady had placed her palm on his forehead and muttered poetic psycho babble religious mutterings. As she spoke an outline of a girl entered his mind. He couldn't pick up all what the old lady had said then and couldn't remember it now but it had been something along the lines of: *she is destined to you, you to her, intertwined by the same strings which tie and vibrate the cosmos, destiny of stars path merging, two galaxies in cosmic dance eating each other alive to become one, sure as light in darkness, and together, you with her, her with you, will be instrumental in the end times, favored of the girl prophet, or if we should fail and all is lost, all will not yet be lost, for you and the girl will be destined to become the new Adam and Eve...* As the old lady spoke the outline of a shape of this girl in Jasper's mind had solidified; she had her bare back turned to him, her skin white and smooth like cream and her shoulder blades made delicate humps carved across her back which her smooth skin snuggly fit over; a line, a slight protrusion which became a slight indent, marked her spine; the shape of her back curving inwards then out at her hips. She held her hair up in a clump over her head with both hands, exposing all the delicate contours and shape and softness of her back. Her arms skinny yet toned, dropped and her hair cascaded down over her back covering what had been exposed. Her hair was dark brown and rippled and fell with the same gentle heaviness of water, Jasper had thought, while under the spell of this vision. As her hair dropped she slightly twisted her torso and began to turn to face him. He thought he caught the sight of the side of her breast (he thought of this a lot afterwards; was he seeing her how she currently was or the women she would be; was she older or the same age?) her chin tucked behind her shoulder; he saw her slightly parted red fleshy lips. But at this moment, right before she turned to face him, allowing him to see all of her, a wall of light had struck him, feeling every bit as physical as any object of solid mass which had ever hit him, which caused him to black out.

He had recurring dreams of this girl ever since. These dreams, he admitted to no one and sometimes had trouble accepting himself, had, sadly, become the best part of his life, despite the frustration of always waking up before having a chance to see what she really looked like, although he could sense with an assurance as clarifying as sight, her beauty. Sometimes in the dreams he heard her voice, but after waking, despite concentrating, he could never quite recall what she sounded like, only knowing it possessed a pleasant chime and that whatever she said comforted him and made him feel warm, full and eager.

There were five other children of the Blue Mangenie cult besides Jasper around the same age as him: three girls, two boys. Two of the girls had crushes on him but he didn't really like either of them. He suspected he was distantly related to them; how closely no one would answer, the subject of blood relation among cult members taboo. He didn't like to think of all the inbreeding; he had no desire to explore his family tree; surly full of a lot of oddballs, like the current parishioners of the cult. He suspected those who claimed psychic ability and who conjured up ghosts and made prophecies and whatnot attributed their "gifts" to this "pure" bloodline of the Blue Mangenie cult/family.

The cult survived only from bloodline, not from proselytizing (they preached secrecy and hiding their existence and beliefs to make it more difficult for the Red Mangenie cult to track them); Jasper suspected it wouldn't survive another generation; a prospect which his father must surely be aware of yet didn't seem concerned about; the cult's mission, its purpose for being, will either have been fulfilled or failed anyways before the next generation comes of age. According to their beliefs anyways, which Jasper no longer prescribed to. Either the world will be saved or doomed, his father and his followers believed, within the next few decades; either way their continuation as a group or organization would no longer matter. If it ever mattered at all, which Jasper was inclined to think it didn't; all this fumbling about and obsessing over some non-existent little girl done because of centuries and generations of built up and pent up delusions.

He heard footsteps climb the basement stairs. He sprang up from his lounging posture and straightened his back. He realized that he had done so from an irrational fear of thinking that his father would equate a couch lounger to a porn watcher in need of some uncomfortable 'you are a vessel to gods light which needs to be kept clean so the light can manifest through you unfiltered; keep your brain pipes unplugged with muck' icky fatherly religious lecture. Like orthodox Catholicism, his father's religion developed some strict morality rules, for some reason Jasper couldn't understand, since hell and heaven were never really discussed too heavily; only 'pleasing the prophesied prophet' who they suspected wouldn't like creeps and immoral pornographers.

He thought about darting to his room to hide from any cult members who might wander up and linger in the kitchen drinking root-beers to save himself from the awkwardness of these people who had known him since a baby, who considered him as family, yet who he disappointed by choosing to no longer formally associating with them. They were coolly polite and sometimes creepily respectful, him being the cult leader's son and all, yet still being around them was uncomfortable. The meetings, usually Sundays and Wednesdays, usually carried on past midnight, and he had always purposefully gone to his room early on those nights, hiding, listening to Radiohead or The Smiths through his earphones, hoping they'd assume he were sleeping. This meeting ended early, it was only 9:45, which caught him by surprise; the basement door would open any moment, someone might catch him trying to dart away, which would just exacerbate the itchy awkwardness between him and the cult; until he was old enough to move away, occasional interactions with his father's cult members was inevitable.

His father was the first to emerge out the door, his followers following behind, as they do. They wore blue silk robes, looking like a gospel choir, although when he had first seen a gospel choir, maybe from some old movie on TV where Whoopi Goldberg pretended to be a nun, he was shocked, thinking there was a chapter of his cult consisting of all black people in the south who publically sang soul music rather than chanted. Jasper had never seen them wear their robes outside of the basement worshiping rooms; in a more ordinary domestic setting they all looked even more ridiculous; silly even, rather than slightly ominously sacred seeming. He then wondered if maybe his father bought these robes from the same catalogs that high school choir teachers bought their robes; but no, these robes were ancient, weren't they, crafted from Chinese silk worms before medieval Italy had even become aware of silk, so his father had once claimed, he recalled.

He looked back at the TV; through his channel surfing he had circled back and stopped back on the game. *Lakers up five. Damn.* Come on Denver. None of the cult members looked at the TV. They kept their hoods up, eyes down, silent, still in solemn worship attitudes. *If I had any friends and one of them barged through the front door right now they'd be seriously creeped out* Jasper thought. A few members couldn't help to raise their eyes to look at him, measuring how much he's grown, as old aunts at summer reunions do. He tried to smile but was unsure how well his mouth obeyed his brain. One of the girls his age who once had a crush on him couldn't help but to linger her gaze over him. Her father gently nudged her back causing her to step forward towards the front door. The cult members emptied out through the front door. Soon only Jasper and his father stood in the living room. A chorus of engines from cult member cars parked along the side streets flared up.

"It's a double full moon in line with Saturn tonight," his father said.

"Oh?" Jasper responded, wondering if his father expected him to know what that means. He still couldn't get over how different the robe looked under white electric light rather than candle light. How... dumb, disturbingly, his dad looked; comical, perhaps were he not his father. The word *sad* entered Jasper's mind.

"We're going to the fields," his father said, again leaving Jasper wondering if his father expected him to know what that means. "To perform a fire ceremony in honor of our rescuer. The psychic Persentine says that the season is near; *by the time the red rose blooms and wilts, all will tilt, towards doom or grace, for the human race.*"

Jasper tired really hard not to roll his eyes. Persentine never was one of their better psychic poets. He couldn't help but feel some embarrassment at seeing his father in such a silly robe, saying such silly words; embarrassed for his father's sake and for his own. He hadn't seen his father wear the robe for nearly three years.

"Come," his father said.

Jasper looked at his shoes then slightly raised his arms and shrugged as he looked back up.

"I still keep ceremonial robes which will fit you," his father informed.

"Dad, I... you know I don't..." Jasper mumbled. He flicked his eyes towards the TV screen to catch Carmelo Anthony hit a reverse layup.

His father pressed his lips tightly together and exhaled through his nose. He flipped his hood back over his head and turned his back to Jasper and walked out the door leaving it open.

CHAPTER FOUR

Cassandra laid tucked tightly in the pink Disney princess comforter in her bed, her head resting on the matching pink pillow, situated in a way where the crown of Sleeping Beauty looked like her own crown, from the perspective of her father looking down on her. He had just finished reading her "Little Red Riding Hood" from a collection which claimed to posses the unsanitized original versions of fairy tales. He didn't know if she were too old for Disney Princesses or fairy tales. She had always been a strange girl; he felt like he had never figured her out. At three years old she would play *Ring Around the Rosie* by herself, languidly spinning around while gently warbling the simple tune with the sinister lyrics: *ashes, ashes, we all fall down.* She played the game as if she knew it were about the bubonic plague, whereas other children played it simply for the hand-holding, twirling, and plopping down fun of it. When Cassandra fell she laid flat and stiff on her back; once her father had feared that she had actually died and crept close to her to peer down at her to see her big eyes wide open and glassy staring absently at the ceiling. She had eyes which seemed to teem with so much vibrant liquid they were in danger of bursting out in tears at any moment. Yet she hardly ever cried; when she did it brought to his mind an icicle melting. She rarely smiled either, yet when she did it made him think her face would crack the way concrete hit by a sledgehammer might. Cassandra's father often watched her with both curiosity and horror. She even ate ice-cream in a way which made him think about death; he couldn't articulate why or how exactly; something about the way she dug the spoon into the dessert made him think of shovels scooping up dirt; the way she'd hold the spoon to her eyes before putting it in her mouth made him think of the heaviness of coldness. At what age had she decided the weight of the world was on her shoulders? By the time she could walk?

"They're all about the loss of innocence you know," Cassandra said.

"What are?" her father asked.

"The fairy tales. The way they originally were. They're meant as warnings of life ahead. Don't stray from the path or you will befall danger. But of course no one can stay a child forever."

Her father lightly chuckled. *Have you ever allowed yourself to be a child, even for a day,* he wondered. He had learned not to probe her on her strangeness. It just seemed to make her sadder. "But they all live happily ever after," he said.

"That's the ending punch line. The ironic twist. The big lie."

Her father forced another chuckle. "I don't know about all that," he said.

"The red of Little Red Riding Hood is symbolic of the blood from the loss of her virginity. If you don't give up your childhood faith in the goodness of people and stray too far into the woods you will be raped. That is the message of Little Red Riding Hood," Cassandra flatly declared.

He didn't watch or listen to the news with her around. He monitored her online activities dutifully; she hardly ever got on the computer. Where'd she learn such words? Would she ever not shock him? He wiped a strand of loose blonde bang off her forehead gently. "But the huntsman comes and kills the wolf," he said. "And the grandmother falls out of the wolf's stomach and is safe."

Cassandra clutched the edge of the blanket and tugged it over her chin. "He shows me rape," she said softly. "One of the many abuses."

Her father sighed heavily. She hadn't brought up 'The Shadow Man' in a long time. He had hoped that she had let go of him, and the Light Man, like letting go of imaginary friends. She was too old for imaginary friends.

"Cassandra... has someone... have you..."

Cassandra closed her eyes. "Not I personally father. But he makes me feel it as if it were me. All the bad." She squeezed her eyes tightly then relaxed them again. "I feel their pain," she whispered.

"Who does?" her father asked although he knew.

"Nothing. No one. Never mind. Daddy, did you love mommy?"

"Of course," he answered. "Why would you ask that?"

"I feel responsible."

"I told you not to."

"I know. Was it fun? To fall in love?"

Her father lightly chuckled and stroked her hair again. "You'll find out someday."

"I won't," she whispered with her eyes closed. "I try..." her voice trailed off.

"I love you. A lot. Do you see... do you feel that?" he asked and placed his palm on her chest over her heart and gently pressed.

"I know you try daddy."

"You've grown so fast."

"I've tasted blood." Her eyes tightened and she turned on her side and let out a whimpering sigh.

"You... what?"

"On our walk to Panda Express. When we passed the homeless man. When he had a daughter, before he lost everything, he'd get drunk and hit her. And he made me feel it."

"I don't understand, who made you... the homeless man?"

"No," Cassandra whispered. "Never mind daddy. It was only a dream. But he wanted to kill her. The daughter. So much hate. So much ugliness. And she wanted to die."

"It was just another bad dream," her father whispered. "You dream of nice things too sometimes? You like telling me the nice things you dream about too, don't you?"

"Light should overpower darkness," Cassandra said.

"That's right," her father answered encouragingly.

"But the darkness has a weight which sinks the soul. The light is unreachable."

"No... no it's not," her father answered, although he didn't know what she were talking about.

"He showed me a family looking at fireworks in Disneyworld. They were happy."

"That's good," her father said. "Just think of that. Go to sleep with that in your mind. Remember, I've saving up. We'll go there someday. Soon."

Cassandra knew he was lying. Not knowingly or purposefully at the moment perhaps; he *intended* to save up money to take her to Disneyworld, except that he couldn't help wasting that money on alcohol and Oxycoton. She didn't completely blame him; he had a hard life and losing his wife during the birth which brought out such a strange and dark daughter, as Cassandra knew herself to be, must be difficult. But his pain would soon leave; he'd soon die, Cassandra knew. Both the Shadow Man and the Light Man had told her.

"We'll go to Disneyworld and the new Harry Potter Land at Universal also, in Orlando, and anyplace else you'd like to go. Sea World to pet the dolphins..."

Cassandra crinkled her nose and shook her head no. Those poor Orca's.

"...The Bahamas, that famous water park there," her father continued. "Dream of those things in your sleep."

Cassandra looked up at him and tried to smile. Her father appreciated her effort but couldn't help but feel a pang of vicarious pain and sadness while looking at her attempt something which seemed so unnatural, to the point of discomfort, for her to try and do.

"It's your birthday next week," her father said.

Cassandra dropped her smile and took her eyes off him, staring at the ceiling.

"Ten years old. Double digits. You're getting so big."

"It's coming closer," Cassandra said still looking at the ceiling, seemingly looking through it up at the stars beyond.

"Yes it is."

"I feel its power in me."

Her father lightly chuckled. "Power of what? Your beauty? You are very pretty you know. Young womanhood? I think you're still a little too young for that... I hope."

"The comet," Cassandra said. "My comet." She usually didn't speak so openly and frankly to her father about the things the shadow man and light man showed her, or about her comet hurling through space towards earth, diverted out of its orbit, towards her like a lost dog running to its master.

"Cassandra..."

"I'm sorry daddy. I'm tired. I'm only sleep talking. Only dreams."

"Do you have friends you'd like to invite to your party?"

"Why do you ask questions you already know the answer to?" Cassandra asked.

She was right, her father knew. He knew she didn't have any friends. He asked if she did because he wished that she did; his question hadn't been sincere but rather his way of telling her he wished she had friends; he wished she were normal; why couldn't she be. He placed his hand on her forehead then removed his hand to kiss just above her right eyebrow.

"Good night daddy. Thanks for the story. I won't wander into the woods alone."

"Good girl," he said. He stood and turned off the lamp on the nightstand near her head. He thought he saw an errant shadow swipe across the wall but he didn't process the sight long enough to try and determine where it had come from; probably caused by headlights from a passing car out the window he guessed, although he hadn't heard any engine, just the same eerie silence which seemed to permeate around Cassandra; even when he played music around her she still sometimes struck him as deaf. He walked out her room and gently swung the door but it slammed shut making the bang noise he had tried to avoid; he guessed it must be due to the wind although he hadn't thought her window open.

Cassandra lay in bed. The Shadow Man came and disturbed her with gory real time images of a man strangling another man to death in a filthy bathroom stall. The Light Man came and showed her the image of a lone tulip protruding from snow on a mountain cliff. She shoved both images away by thinking of her comet. She heard the combustible rumblings sounding like billowing fire roaring in a furnace caused by the rocky ice layers of the comet melting and breaking free joining the flowing tail which elongated further the closer it came towards the sun. The sound and shake and power of the comet increased with each second it hurled towards the sun at an unfathomable speed. She heard and felt her beautiful comet, the size of Texas. She couldn't help but smile, for real, not forced, at feeling the force of its power; the pleasure shook all other thoughts and emotions away and dominated her with internal shakings. In moments of feeling the power of her comet she became powerless to it. To merely let all that power pass by unused seemed impossible to her; to feel the majestic cosmic trembling shake her insides and vibrate her lips, and then to use those same lips to say to it, no, you must pass by without impact, felt too great a burden to her. Yet she knew she must, somehow, if the world were to be spared. But in feeling the power of the comet she could do nothing but to surrender to it and let it shake out all doubts and troubles and uncertainties, to become the only force in her, simple and straight, barreling ahead; she tightened her body in anticipation of the collision and her unconscious smile let out a giggle.

CHAPTER FIVE

Cassandra's father bought angel food cake for her, slathered in pink cool whip frosting. He placed it in front of her as she sat at the head of the tiny wood table in the kitchen. He took out his cigarette lighter from his pocket and used it to light the candles. He looked at her and wished she would smile rather than look so frozen and comatose, even more than usual for her he thought; he wanted her to smile, even if it meant that her face would crack, even if it'd be insincere, just smile why don't you, he thought. She flickered her eyes to the side then looked ahead again, gazing absent mindedly at nothing, lost in her internal melancholy reverie. Her father breathed out his nose. *People's attitudes and demeanors are contagious* he thought, *and her dourness has rubbed on me and any energetic cheerfulness I've feigned has not seeped into her at all. I'm just going to give up soon. She has sunk me; I have failed to raise her up.* He cleared his throat and began to warble *Happy Birthday* but stopped himself after the second *To You.*

"Cassandra, babe, I'm not much of a singer. Why don't you help me out? ...Even though it's your birthday."

Cassandra flickered her eyes on him in a way which seemed inhuman to him; how she could so languidly, absent-mindedly stare off into space; how she moved slow like she were under water, to then snap so quickly with the instincts of a startled deer; or how a lizard will lay stiff and frozen on a red rock under the sun to then slither away quick as a snake strike at the sound of a broken twig. It spooked him. His own daughter unnerved him. He cleared his throat. He looked at her eyes, so large and seemingly ready to break and burst into tears, if only they would unfreeze. He forced a chuckle. "It's your birthday."

She went back to staring straight ahead. Then she looked into the candle flames. The red-orange glow reflected off her eyes. *Happy Birthday to you* her father again warbled. In the flames she saw a large redwood pine burning, the red sparks and ashes rising up and being carried by the wind; little floating flame seeds. Destruction is so much faster than building. How long has it taken for these trees to grow hundreds of feet tall? How quickly they burn and fall. In her vision the redwood trees became New York City skyscrapers; the Chrysler building, the Empire State building, ablaze with the same ferocity as if they were made of wood not steel. The red blazes tumbling from the towers were not embers but people. All matter becomes ash through fire. She heard the cackling of the Shadow Man and then saw his shadow excitedly racing and dancing across the walls with sinister glee.

"Cassandra," her father said. "The song's over. Time to make your wish. Blow out the candles."

What to wish for Cassandra wondered. *I wish to make the right decision. Whether to save everything or destroy everything.* She blew on the flames. Instead of her breath extinguishing the fire her breath caused the flames to burst as if she spit at them with gasoline. Her breath on tiny flame caused an instant explosion, spreading flames out and licking the walls, ceiling, furniture, her father, at once. Cassandra gasped in surprise and horror. She knew perilous and horrific moments would happen, including the death of her father, but didn't know when or how or that'd she'd be the direct cause.

"Dad!" she screamed and looked ahead and saw the blackened shape of a crouched man engulfed in flame. The man, her father, turned and ran towards the front door, not far off because of the smallness of the house. He crashed through the front door made flimsy from the heat. "Dad!" Cassandra yelled again and ran towards him. She realized that the flames did not attach to her and she did not feel heat; to her it was as if the flames were only her continued illusion. She ran out the house and saw her father as a crackling lump of burning limbs on the front lawn. She looked out and across the street and saw the silent scream through a large living room window of their neighbor, the old widow Mrs. Lancaster; her eyes bulging, her jaw hung open, stretching her shriveled skin over her face while the lose skin flaps below her chin, on her neck, sagged and swayed. *Hideous* Cassandra thought. She looked back down at her father. "Help" he squeaked. "Light Man, help me."

A wind blew over her which extinguished the flames on her father but not the flames destroying the house behind her. She looked down and saw a smoldering blackened and crisped skeletal corpse where her father had been. She looked at the smoke rising hoping to see his soul rise, wishing to speak with him and tell him she's sorry, for everything, tell him this was an accident, she didn't mean it, thank him for the cake and for always trying so hard to make her happy, buying her the dolls and dresses, the bedtime stories and hugs and kisses, in the constant frustrating and futile effort to try to make her happy and more like a normal child; sorry for being me and killing you; sorry for not being normal. She looked at the rising smoke but didn't see his spirit rise. Through the smoke she saw Mrs. Lancaster peering at her through her living room window. The old widow screamed again and closed the blinds once she saw Cassandra peering at her.

Cassandra grit her teeth and squeezed her eyes shut and felt two hot tears run down her cheek. "He was a good man," she heard the Light Man say.

"No human in flesh form can be good," she heard the Shadow Man declare. "He didn't love you. He was frightened of you. He only loved his hopeless dreams and his alcohol."

"He did love you," The Light Man said. "He just didn't understand your burdens. No one does."

"Where will I go now?" Cassandra asked through her tears.

"The time has come. The comet soon approaches," the Light and Shadow men said in unison.

Cassandra heard the siren screams of the county emergency vehicles coming closer.

CHAPTER SIX

Cassandra walked directly across the street and knocked on Mrs. Lancaster's door. The old lady ducked and skirmished to the corner of her living room and hugged her knees, cowering. She squeezed her cross necklace so tight the end points painfully pierced into the flesh of her palms. She squeezed her eyes shut and fervently prayed through her whimpering: *please god make the demon child leave and not harm me.* The line became a religious mantra repeated.

Cassandra's shadow man friend kicked the old lady's front door open and raced into the house cackling, his shadow dancing across her walls. An unnatural wind flowed in behind him. Cassandra stood in the open doorway. Mrs. Lancaster peeked and saw Cassandra standing in her open doorway with wind billowing up behind her head causing her hair to flow and wave as if under the ocean; the light of the flames from the burning house behind Cassandra illuminated the outline of her hair and her eyes seemed also to glow. Mrs. Lancaster shrieked and ducked her head back into her knees and couldn't feel the pain from the edges of her white gold cross necklace breaking through the dry skin of her bony hands.

"Demon child! I knew you were a demon child! Stay away from me!" Mrs. Lancaster shrieked with her eyes still shut.

Cassandra took a step into the house towards the old lady who flinched and whimpered from the sound of the footstep. "Tell them the time is near," Cassandra directed in a loud monotone voice to be heard over the flames and sirens. "Tell them the girl prophet has emerged and she will soon make her decision. Tell the dumb Red and Blue Mangenie families to come search for me if they believe they have a hand in fate."

Cassandra turned and walked out the door leaving Mrs. Lancaster huddled in her corner like a mouse with burned paws. The old lady kept in her corner as she heard the blaring sirens increase louder, so loud she plugged her ears with her hands. Even with her eyes closed she could see, as a sense, the orange lights of the blaze next door, then the rotating blue and red strobe lights of the fire engines, police cars and ambulance. She still saw the mental image of the demon child standing in her doorway, both her hair and eyes alive and aflame, overflowing with supernatural frightening powers. She heard a knock on her door and she whimpered again, flinching.

"Mam," she heard a firm but kindly gentleman's voice say. "Your door was open. Are you all right?"

The old lady cautiously opened her eyes and saw a police officer leaning through her doorway. She unclasped her cross and opened her hands and noticed blood spots on her palms. "Stigmata! Stigmata!" she shrieked. "Jesus saved me, praise god!"

"Mam? Excuse me?" the police officer said. "May I come in?"

"The demon child," the lady yelled. "She set her house on fire, an explosion, her poor daddy, she killed him! Burned on the front lawn right before my eyes; an unholy fire! Then she came over and she... she... threatened me!"

Mrs. Lancaster then began to cry. The police officer entered, walked towards her, bent down and comfortingly placed his hand over her shoulder to try and steady her shaking.

Mrs. Lancaster still hadn't calmed down by the time the local channel 5 news arrived, live on the scene for a live report, and agreed to give an eye-witness account to the reporter. Her mind raced once she stood next to the local celebrity reporter; the camera light shined in her eyes and a man behind the man holding the camera counted down from five and then the reporter lady spoke about a West Valley fire and a casualty, words which sounded muffled to Mrs. Lancaster and then Mrs. Lancaster found the microphone in front of her mouth. "The demon child, she had no eyes, they were black then they glowed, she set the house on fire, an explosion like a hellfire bomb, then she burned her father and said the end time is nigh, the Mangenie family, find her, kill her!" the old lady frantically shrieked, her voice rising, eyes bulging, fingers curled near her face, giving off the impression of a hysterical lunatic.

The reporter quickly jerked the microphone away and hoped the lights hid her blushing. Humiliated, she worried her bosses would reprimand her for this on air fiasco; she should have screened this crazy lady before putting her on air. She smirked before sending it back to Dan in the studio who mimicked her smirk and said flippantly "you heard it here first" while his co-anchor Linda tried to hide her nervous grimace through shuffling papers and giggling.

A day later a young local viewer uploaded the clip of the old crazy lady on his YouTube channel, titling it *Crazy Old Lady Freaks Out, The End Of the World Is Near!!!* About a week after the video was posted it began to go viral on the merits of the comedy in seeing an old bug-eyed lady freak out on live television, screeching nonsense about a demon child with dark and glowing eyes who apparently set her house on fire, followed by the chirpy *Back to you Dan* sign off from the befuddled unintentionally smiling pretty news reporter.

A comedy blog Jasper sometimes frequented called *Best Week Ever* posted the video on their site. Jasper sat in front of the computer Tuesday morning, a bowl of Fruity Pebbles next to the keyboard. He had checked his Facebook page, Twitter and Google News and still had time to kill before heading to school so he checked out comedy blogs, including *Best Week Ever.* Coincidently, the video of the old lady had been their most recent post, residing at the top of the page. He scanned the headline: *Local News Reports Demon Child on the Lose!* He glanced at the video freeze of the old lady with bugged eyes, clawed fingers and white bristly fro hair. He smirked a laugh with a spoonful of pink milk and cereal in his mouth. He clicked on the video and the old lady moved and spoke; Jasper couldn't help but to laugh though his nose just at the silliness of her high pitched screeching voice and melodramatic gestures.

The video lasted thirty two seconds. Jasper stared at the screen, silent, a bite of cereal soggy in his mouth, unable to swallow. His mind felt chilled. He wondered why he wasn't laughing. This was hysterical after all. Crazy lady saying crazy things; always funny. Right? Except when it's sad. ...Or... if her crazy ramblings sound too familiar. He heard a word he recognized that no one but a few others should know. He wondered if he should play it again to confirm he had heard what he thought he heard but found that he couldn't; doing so would be like reopening a closet door where a moment before he had seen a ghost. Maybe the ghost was still there but he didn't want to find out; let it remain invisible; if it is ignored does it exist? He forced himself to swallow. He looked at the screen capture of the old lady who had so quickly been transformed from comical to terrifying. She had spoken the cult's family name. Did she say the girl... What had she mentioned of a girl? Could she really have been referring to... could there actually be some truth in... If he were asked to speak he would have been unable to; even his thoughts were stuttering, unable to finish the sentences. *Could it all be true?* He couldn't process the weight of that question. He thought even if he showed this video to his father (should he?) even his father would be surprised; even among the most faithful and spiritual, there is a line that separates perceived reality from theological abstract dogmas, among the semi-sane anyways. *But really, should I show this to my father,* he wondered, the question hitting him like a soft jab in his abs.

"Jasper are you still here? You'll be late for school," he heard his father yell from the study room.

Jasper realized he would be late for school if he didn't leave that very moment; he'd probably be late anyways, and he must snap himself out of his frozen daze; just throw all these questions away for the moment; just pretend this crazy old lady had never come up. He reached for the mouse and with a shaky hand, fumbling in his haste, placed the curser over the X in the right corner and clicked, closing the blog, revealing the screen saver, a picture of his dead mother, smiling during a sunset on an Oregon beach.

CHAPTER SEVEN

Janelle laid in bed in the evening listening to the rain splatter her window, walls and ceiling. The rain beat down steady which made a white noise she thought would lull her to sleep but instead the sound lubricated her reverie, causing her thoughts to pour out fast and fall languidly, like rain pouring into deepening puddles which overfill and run down rain gutters. She felt tired and stimulated, bored and engaged with her unfocused random thoughts. She enjoyed the sound of rain and usually welcomed it; she'd lived in this costal Oregon town for nearly six months and it rained a lot. She sometimes pretended she had moved to the same sleepy rainy town as Bella Swan did in Twilight (the teen romance Vampire series) and soon something exciting might happen to her, the same way it did to Bella, meeting her sensitive and gorgeous vampire soul mate. But she knew she'd most likely soon move before anything exciting would happen; she moved a lot. So for now, enjoy the rain. It would be the symbol of this place she moved to, she decided. She picked a symbol for each place to encapsulate her memories and impressions: a dolphin for Savannah Georgia, an arrowhead for Tulsa Oklahoma, a Shamrock for Boston, a wad of gum stuck to a seashell for San Lucas Obistbo California, now rain for Newport Oregon. Or a gray whale; she hadn't decided. She had lived in New York as a six year old a decade ago when the 2001 terrorist attacks had happened, the hijacked planes used as missiles crashing into the twin towers. She didn't need a symbol to remember New York.

She thought of the Civil War. It's the 150th anniversary. She wondered if the South *still* doesn't wish they had won. As strange as that is to comprehend. The blood stains of the war still wash over us. The propaganda, racism, politics, still echoes, still influences what's happening now; to discuss it is to inevitably cause arguments, from 'states rights' to 'gun rights' and 'heritage' and hate and everything.

The past is part of us. We are born into it. If 'we', 'you', 'people' were born into a rich plantation family in the Antebellum South, 'we', 'you' 'people' would have most likely been a racist, with all the ugliness being attached to that immoral repugnant philosophy entails, from birth to death. Could it have been helped? If you were born a Muslim in Iran to a terrorist father, you may be more inclined to think Al-Qaeda has some good points, possibly, as impossible as that is to comprehend. Isn't that strange.

Her father, at the moment, conducted one of his crazy cult meetings in their basement. He considered himself the leader of this tiny nomadic cult calling themselves the Red Mangenie family. Other than that he appeared as a nice normal guy to the outside world. A casual acquaintance would never suspect he led some cult who traveled all over the country, directed by the whims of these cult psychics in search of some girl who they believe they needed to kill in order to bring about gods wishes and ways and destiny and path for the world and humankind.

Even as a child she had always thought the tenants of the cult she was born into strange. She believed if she had been born in the antebellum south, she still wouldn't have been a pro-slavery racist, and if she were born in Iran she wouldn't believe in terrorism. She didn't believe it right to go out searching for some "demon child" or "false prophet girl" to "scourge" (murder) in order to not disrupt the flow of nature, or whatever. That's crazy, no matter where you're from or what language you speak. Still, just being sixteen she had to travel with her father. She came to see the cult as quaint and harmless, just misguided. Now, if they really did murder some poor little girl, that'd change things, but she didn't believe they ever really would follow through on their threats; there was no "demon girl" anyways. She was grateful that her father allowed her to make her own decisions, unlike other cult children she'd heard about who are 'thrown out' and become homeless if they choose not to believe. Although as a child she had been tattooed with the cult emblem on her back, on her right shoulder, not really against her will but at four years old she didn't really know what her will was, or that she possessed such a thing. She still cringes when thinking about the pain of the inked needle repeatedly poking through her skin.

Her thoughts continued to unspool (movies, music, celebrities, [she watched a "Fashion Police" episode right before crawling into bed] fashion, love, school, the future, nature, the rain) to a point where it annoyed her she was still awake and wished to submerge and transfer her random thoughts into dreams.

She heard a soft knock on her door. "Are you still awake?" her father asked.

"Yes," she answered.

Her father entered. Janelle sat up and brushed her fingers through her bangs. She noticed by the light in the hallway creeping in through her half ajar door that her father still wore his blood red silky ceremonial robe and she couldn't help but roll her eyes and utter a breathy grunt.

"You just can't help being a teenager can you?" he teased. "Always embarrassed by me."

"What do you want dad?"

"Did you hear about the riots in Egypt?" he asked.

"Yeah. It's a crazy world. Always has been."

"It's prophecy fulfilled. The dominos are lined up."

"Dad... we've talked about this. You know how I feel." She thought: *Besides, you know I can't take you seriously when you're wearing that goofy robe.*

"Yes. But you know I'll never stop trying. Or stop asking."

Janelle rolled her eyes again. "I know dad." She knew his persistence of trying to get her to rejoin the cult was at least done out of love and concern for her, despite her thinking he were simply confused and wrong in his cult beliefs, annoying and discomforting as his persistence and resulting "talks" were. She rested her chin in her raised knees, subconsciously recoiling and tightening away from her father, hating seeing him in his robe, hating even more these father-daughter talks meant to be meaningful and serious, but always resulting in agonizing quietly held torture.

"How about you join us next time. The time is near," her father said.

"Noooo thanks," Janelle replied semi-sarcastically while trying to hold off a guffaw.

"Analessa..."

"One of the psychics?" Janelle asked, interrupting, pretending not to know.

"You know Analessa... ever since you were little..."

"Whatever," Janelle said.

"She's predicted you'll play an important role. Janelle, the fate of the world..."

Janelle sighed. She thought: *Yeah dad, I know; important stuff, the fate of the world hinges in the balance, destroy the doomsday impeder, blah, blah, blah; but it doesn't mean anything if you don't believe in it; it's all a myth, same as all the crazy ideas people believe about the Aztec calendar predicting the end of the world in 2012, or all that crazy science fiction Scientology crap about evil space lord what's-his-name, some wacky celebs take as fact because they claim this belief cured their dyslexia, or whatever.*

Cassandra's father let out his own sigh of exasperation. "Did you read the article I gave you yet?"

"About the teen brain? How it's like a new Ferrari... shiny, fast, sexy, sleek, but with bad breaks?"

"Yeah, that's the one."

Janelle shrugged. "I just skimmed it. Why'd you want me to read it anyways?"

Her father shrugged back. "Just found it interesting... How are you doing with school?"

Janelle gave him a *are you serious* blank stare for a few seconds before saying: "dad... please. We can't have this conversation with you dressed like... that... so go continue your sacrificial rituals or whatever."

Her father forced a chuckle. "Have you made any new friends?"

Janelle lowered her nose into her knees and looked where her blanket covered her toes.

"Are we moving again?" she mumbled, not looking up.

"You know I'm not worried about you. Cheryl says..."

"Cheryl?"

"Our top psychic."

"I thought that was Analeesa."

"If you'd come to our meetings sometimes, you'd know..."

"Anyways dad, I have to sleep."

"They both say you'll have an important role to play in bringing down Bezzandra." ("Bezzandra" was one of the dopier names they gave the prophet girl).

"You have a hundred names for her," Janelle mumbled. "It's weird."

"Honestly, I don't see it," her father said, nudging her shoulder playfully.

"Dad!" Janelle shot back, but then confused herself trying to figure out why she should be offended that her father had doubts concerning her supposed importance in a false religion anyways.

Her father lightly chuckled. "But faith is following what you can't automatically see. Our psychics have been right about so many things already."

"Except being able to pin-point where exactly this girl is for some reason, so we crisscross all over the country like nomads or gypsies or something."

"It's complicated. The psychics of the Blue Mangenie family are strong as well and they muddle..."

"Muddle?" Janelle asked, interrupting.

"Yes, muddle."

"Muddle," Janelle said. "You don't hear that word very often. Muddle. So, like, psychic warfare or something?"

"Something like that," her father said, thinking, *Muddle is a common word. I thought you liked to read. Just how badly is your education suffering, moving around so much. Or, are you just messing with me? I never know with you.*

"If our psychics are so good why don't they use their *powers...*" (Janelle said the word while rolling her eyes and flexing her fingers into quote gestures) "... to bet on sports games and junk."

After a pause her father looked down, tugged his robe then said, "how do you think we afford everything?"

Janelle stared at him blankly for a moment then said, "you're kidding."

He shrugged in response.

"I thought you were like a... stock broker, or banker, or investor or something like that."

"Yes, we do that too."

"...I don't mean for this to come out wrong but... so like, why aren't we richer? Bet a million dollars on the Super Bowl you know?"

"We don't have that much..."

"I mean, work up to it..."

"We use the gifts only with prudence, only when necessary, to provide adequate sustenance for..."

"Dad," Janelle interrupted. "Just, whatever." She flopped back down in her bed and pulled the covers over her head. "Dad? She mumbled. So this will all be over soon, you think? All the traveling, the robes... the... everything?"

"You feel it too?" her father said sounding almost grossly eager. "The time is near. It's racing so fast the earth is shaking, trembling, like a bubbling volcano before it blows. I know you can feel it too."

Janelle sighed. "Whatever daddy."

Her father left. She signed again. God, she hoped they didn't go out and seek and kill some poor little girl. God, if they did that... what would she do. She'd have to call the police or something, she decided, thinking about the Civil War and Muslim terrorists. She lamented that she didn't have any friends, never had a boyfriend, her life just a series of spider silk strands strung to and fro, fragile, blown away in the morning wind, nothing attached.

CHAPTER EIGHT

Jasper and his father's cult moved to Salt Lake City the day after the world was supposed to end/the rapture was supposed to take place, according to a geriatric Bay Area doomsday prophet and preacher (self proclaimed) who had about fifty followers (about twenty five more than Jasper's father's cult). Jasper had gotten a kick from reading the "End of the World" jokes on twitter and online: *don't worry, it's not the end of the world, well that was anti-climatic,* type of things. Despite the glibness, real people had been hurt by this false prophet's false prediction; a man spent his fortune on billboards advertising the end date in New York; cameras were on him in Times Square during the moment of his supposed ascension into heaven and he just stood there, arms out, looking up, until the joke just became sad. Still, he said his faith has not been shook; the Bible Code has been cracked, he was just being tested. Some family had taken their children out of school and rented an RV and preached the end date at national parks and amusement park parking lots. Another follower had set himself on fire in the middle of the Golden Gate Bridge after the day had passed, thinking, apparently, it's what god told him to do in order to get into heaven. *How can people be so crazy,* Jasper thought. *Religion turns people insane; just look at The Middle East and our own climate denying, war mongering, science-impaired strain of Christianity in the USA.*

The next week the preacher declared he had miscalculated; a spiritual judgment had occurred that day which he had prophesied the world would end, sweeping over the world, rolling in at the six O'clock hour, and the physical part, the punishments from the judgments, would come next October. He still has believers who believe what he says, who feel empowered that god had tested their faith, yet still they believe. Reality will not penetrate their delusions.

Jasper went to the first day at his new school. It was the same school they had used for the "High School Musical" Disney Channel movies which had become a cultural phenomenon awhile ago; a fact the school still proudly apparently trumpeted, with a "High School Musical" gift shop on campus, which Jasper thought sort of sad and strange: the power of the cultural force of the thing was limp now; who even will remember it in another year or so? He sat in a wood chair in the school office in front of the secretary's counter, waiting to go into the principal's office. He knew the new kid introduction routine. He looked at the clock on the wall and the American flag in the corner, wondering which stars belonged to which States.

"I'm sorry, we're waiting for another transfer student to arrive," the secretary said, then looked past Japer and said "well speak of the devil."

In walked a girl. "Hello, I'm Janelle," she said.

"Please take a seat, I'll tell the principle you've arrived," the secretary said.

"Thank you," Janelle said and sat next to Jasper.

As she sat next to him he felt an electric jolt run up his spine. He turned to look at her without trying to gawk at her. Her lips were strawberry red. Her skin soft and white. He had an urge to see her naked back; an urge which titillated and embarrassed him; he had to mentally tell himself not to be a creep. She giggled, looking down at her iPhone screen.

***

Cassandra lay on the top of a grassy hill in Sugar House Park in the chilly night air looking up at the stars. She hadn't eaten in three days but didn't feel hungry; she had only really eaten before to please her father.

She felt alien. She sometimes felt like an all powerful god and other times like a perplexed tourist. Nothing ever internalized, feelings only vicarious. She didn't understand how people could fall in love, but thought it nice when they did. She didn't know which was more correct: bright youthful optimism or brittle old person's fatalism. The

Light Man showed her the selfless acts of men, the Shadow Man showed her selfish acts; she didn't know which held more power over the world, but it seemed to tip more towards selfishness; a lack of empathy, tribalism, greed. Are we all like dying fish in dry river beds flopping under the sun desperate for air, for meaning, for anything, when nothing is to be taken but death, she wondered.

CHAPTER NINE

Janelle and Jasper had English class together. The subject was Romeo and Juliet again, the most overrated, over taught play ever, Jasper thought. But of course it contains some good lines.

These violent delights have violent ends and in their triumph die, like fire and powder, which As they kiss consume. What do you think that means, the teacher asked.

Janelle raised her hand and the teacher called on her. "That passion is like a candle burning at two ends," she answered. "That the same stuff that causes the thrill can lead to the destruction."

"Good," the teacher said. "And do you think the thrill is worth it then, if it simply leads to destruction?"

"Sure, I guess," Janelle said. "I mean *it is better to have loved and lost than never had loved at all,* right? Is that from Shakespeare also?"

"Well I just think it's hot," some other girl interjected. "It's totally about orgasm." The class collectively giggled. Janelle shot Jasper a look then bit her lip smiling. Jasper looked away, blushing.

Janelle and Jasper both tried out for the school play. It was a student written drama about the end of the world. The Apocalypse had become something of a cultural trend, with all the Young Adult Dystopian novels and movies based on them and the hysterics of politicians fear mongering. Perhaps the still struggling economy and war quagmires dragging like a stone noose around America's neck brought on this more depressing cultural trend, far less bright than the 'High School Musical' stuff of a half decade or so ago. Still, we party on.

This student's play took place in the near future, December of 2012, two and a half years away, (*Isn't it always strange when the 'future date' of a old work of fiction comes and passes,* Jasper had thought, flipping through the script; *it's why using dates in fiction about the future should be avoided; although, using 2012 is understandable, since the Aztec Calendar supposedly predicts the world will end then; that's a cultural meme going around; and I guess an 'artist' or whatever, really should write for the present even when they're imagining a future*). The two leads of this play, because of some genetic mutation in them (or fate) survive the disease which killed everyone else, and all the play mostly consists of is just these two teens, the new Adam and Eve, talking about junk. It was a very good play, even for a student written endeavor, but the playwright, a nebbish kid named Doug, was too young to realize just how bad it was, and in his mind he had written something cutting edge and extraordinary, which delved into the depths of human psyche and skillfully addressed weighty issues of loneliness, love, death, sadness, fear, euphoria, guilt (the guilt the girl protagonist eventually feels for feeling euphorically in love and strangely happy despite the seven billion deaths) sex and simply *everything*. Religion, and *everything*. The author thought he'd one day be an award winning Broadway playwright who'd move on to movie scripts and be rich and celebrated, houses in Hawaii and France. Sure, he knew his work wasn't perfect, but he believed it to be a first bold step, and of course, *important*.

Jasper and Janelle got the leads. The playwright liked that they were both new and unknown and that their *out of place* feelings, being transfer students who've traveled all over (both military brats, they claimed; the only plausible excuse a kid could have for having moved so much and attended so many different schools) would help their performances. Also they both just happened to be really good looking and also happened to look really good together. And they had an immediate *chemistry;* a type which really can't be acted or forced, but just simply must be, in order to be. They were rough around the edges, like his play, but he would mold them.

After Friday rehearsal Janelle drove Jasper home in her red Ford Mustang.

"Who is this?" Jasper asked, referring to the music.

"The Cults," Janelle answered.

Jasper chuckled.

"Why is that funny?"

"Oh, it's not. I don't know," he answered. "I like this song. Is it called 'run away'?"

"Good guess," Janelle answered. "But actually no. It's called 'Bad Things.'"

Run, run, run away and never come back, the female singer sweetly sung in a charming cute voice.

They talked more about the music. The sweet voiced girl singing songs with eerie troubling lyrics about running away from a cult, being infatuated, wanting to go outside, walk at night, feeling things deeply, too deeply, dangerously. Nice simple pleasant melodies masking some troubling themes. *I'm afraid of the light; do you know what I mean,* goes a lyric.

They talked about Emma Roberts; she was in a "Cults" video and Jasper had recently seen her in a video hobnobbing at a Sundance premier after party after a screening of one of her indie movies, and she bumped up, literally, against this cute guy in a really friendly and cool way.

Drifting from my family, the 'Cults' singer sang; Jasper asked if he heard that right, Janelle said she thinks so. The songs were short.

"Have you ever thought about running away?" Jasper asked.

"Just about every day," Janelle answered. "You?"

"Well, why?"

"It's complicated I guess," Janelle said. "So what do you think of this play we're doing?"

"Pretty much crap," Jasper said.

Janelle laughed. "Yeah, pretty much my assessment also."

"But it's kind of fun I guess... the character. Last man on earth or whatever."

"Let's cheese ball it up. It's so earnest, right? It'd be fun to just take it over the top."

Jasper thought of the kissing scenes. They hadn't actually kissed practicing those scenes yet.

"You don't think Doug would notice or care?" (Doug, the wonder kid playwright).

"You kid, right? Gawd, that guy is so pretentious. His head is so far up his butt."

"Totally," Jasper said.

Janelle turned the sound up for her favorite song, *Walk at night.* She likes the piano tinkling break down part.

They talked about Jackie Evancho, Chloe Moretz, Beatniks and the term 'you're so square'. Janelle pulled up to his house. "See you tomorrow."

Jasper walked through his door. His father bombarded him with new reports of impending doom: a Seattle Earthquake set to strike at any moment, killing millions; the Yellowstone Cauldron could be as impactful as the earth being struck by a meteor when it explodes; it could blow as soon as now. Jasper quickly ate the warm spaghetti and meatballs, from a can, his father had microwaved and went to his room. Sort of stupid, he thought, to care about school and homework, if the world is ending any moment now, but whatever. He looked over his math homework then worked on memorizing lines for the play, while listening to his Pandora online music station. He checked Twitter; what do the young celebrities have to say? What selfies have they recently taken? What excites them? What are they promoting now, other than themselves.

Pandora played "Breath Me" by Sia. The trancelike translucent beautiful song made him think of Janelle. So edgy, brave, bold, so long yet petite, not grossly long, a long neck; usually he liked short girls, he thought, but then realized he hadn't ever really liked anyone before; there was nothing, only silly meaningless crushes, before Janelle. Janelle was everything.

**

Cassandra lived as a homeless girl. She usually slept in the tunnel linking Sugar House Park to the nature trail and shopping area; a two story Barnes and Noble nearby, a Panda Express restaurant and Old Navy cloths store. She would sometimes sneak onto the Trax line to ride downtown to get free soup. She'd wash herself in the manmade lake at the park at nights. The Shadow Man and Light Man protected her. She looked nearly skeletal. Whenever a case worker or random stranger or whoever tried to intervene with her to try and help her she'd scare them away by telling them their secrets and visions of the end of the world.

**

Janelle came to Jasper's house Saturday evening to work on lines from the play.

Doomsday Now was the name of the play. The main characters were named Mack and Lacy. They worked on this scene:

Mack: Everything's gone. Gone, gone, gone. Hopeless. No internet service. No television.

Lacy: Are you kidding? Billions of people have just died and all you care about is no internet or TV?

Mack: Well... I get bored. Don't you get bored?

Lacy: my mother is dead! My father is dead! My sisters, June, April, and little May, all dead!

Mack: So why is your name Lacy?

Lacy: What do you mean?

Mack: All your other sisters are named after months.

Lacy: Oh, shut up. Stop trying to be funny. How can you be funny in a time like this?

Mack: Well everyone dies eventually. It's only a matter of time when.

Lacy: How can you say that? How can you be so callous?

Mack: Look... I mean, what can we do? Kill ourselves? What good would that do.

Lacy: I do want to kill myself actually.

Mack: Don't say that. We might be the only two humans left alive for all we know.

Lacy: I... I don't want to believe that.

Mack: Look around. Do you see anyone else?

Lacy: I don't want that pressure! Or that responsibility!

Mack: Well we're not going to rebuild the world in a day. Our responsibility is rather simple and straightforward actually.

Lacy: What do you mean?

Mack: Well... we're young. We have good genes; we didn't get the disease that killed off everyone else.

Lacy: Yes, unfortunately.

Mack: the human race, the continuation of our species depends on us. All we have to do is procreate and we'll be like... the saviors of mankind, right? I mean, we'll freak'n be like Adam and Eve; our children's children's children will write stories about us that will become the new books of religion.

Lacy: No, don't be blasphemous. If it weren't for Adam and Eve we wouldn't be here, and they were created by god. It still goes back to them, back to god, being the creator.

Mack: God? Look around. All the destruction; all the death, billions, everyone, and you still talk about god?

Lacy: sex, sex, sex, that's all boys think about!

Mack: Well what else do you want to do? What's the best cure for boredom? We can't sit around just looking at the ash filled sky all day; can't really play video games or watch Wipeout on ABC on Tuesdays, or American Idol or X Factor or Jimmy Fallen or...

Lacy: Wow, you watched a lot of TV.

Mack: And now I can't anymore! All my internet friends are dead as well. Every idiot on the IMDB message boards... I hated them but I never wished them to be dead!

Lacy: Well how can you be horny in a time like this?

Mack: How can I not be!

Lacy: Books. I'm sure there are some books around; some libraries that survived the fires. There's enough books already written to occupy a handful of lifetime's worth. Billions of books. I could just read the Harry Potter series over and over, or the Hunger Games trilogy, and Twilight and... the classics, Jane Austin's stuff, Hemmingway; I've never read him besides the book about the fish for school and I never really got into The Great Gatsby but it's considered a classic so I could try that again, and The Mortal Instruments series and... Just billions of books. Jack Kerouac... It's too bad they never finished The Hunger Games movie...

Mack: Ugh, will you please stop talking?

Lacy: And then there's 'The Diary of a Wimpy Kid' series for you.

Mack: Maybe there's a stack of Playboys left somewhere...

Lacy: Ugh, you're disgusting.

Mack: Well, if you won't give me anything. A man has needs you know.

Lacy: You're not a man, you're just a boy.

Mack: Which makes it worse.

Lacy: You don't need electricity to enjoy a book. There's nothing to plug in. Whole new worlds and people to discover. We could memorize favorite passages from books and recite them to each other. Put on little plays.

Mack: (sarcastically) Well you're a barrel of fun.

The play continued that way; just mostly Mack and Lacy talking about nothing. Then near the end they have sex, although the stage direction is vague: *Lacy and Mack walk hand in hand around a rock and have sex by a running stream.* Jasper and Janelle joked and laughed over how they would play and rehearse that scene. Maybe go around a rock and simulate sex sounds, moaning and panting, building the climax. Or go straight stage porn and do it for real on stage; wouldn't that be the scandalous shocker, here in Salt Lake City, Mormon town.

"Does Doug intend this to be funny?" Janelle asked.

"I don't know. But it is pretty funny, the absurdity of it. But no, I think he thinks he's written the most serious important work ever."

Janelle laughed. "But we'll play it funny."

"In a way in which Doug won't even know we're making fun of him or his work," Jasper added.

"Totally," Janelle said then laughed again. "*Oh Mack, but there are books! Books Mack, that don't need electricity to be read!*" Janelle said in an overheated melodramatic way, mocking the original dialogue.

"*But sex! Sex, and there's no television, no Gossip Girl, no Vampire Diaries, no Wipeout on ABC on Tuesdays, so we must have sex!*" Jasper said, playing along in the spoof.

"Yes, but we have Harry Potter. We can just read Harry Potter to each other, over and over, forever, and reenact the parts. I'll be Dumbledore you be Harry."

"Dead, dead, dead, everything's dead! All my favorite TV shows! Agh, I hate you!"

"But we'll always have Harry Potter!"

Janelle and Jasper burst in laughter, unable to maintain their characters.

"You know, some say the Aztecs said the world will end in 2012. Their calendar ends then or something," Janelle said.

"Yeah, there's a whole market now trying to get money off of it, with books and junk. The Aztecs were crazy though," Jasper said.

"They knew a lot about stars, apparently. Astronomy and stuff. More than the Europeans at the time, who were supposedly more advanced," Janelle said.

"Yeah, but all the human sacrifice of young virgins. I mean... gross."

"Yeah, that's true," Janelle said with a dismissive shrug. She gazed at a painting of a desert landscape, particularly drawn to the image of the purple lizard painted on the red boulder.

"Are you hungry?" Jasper asked.

"Yeah, sort of."

"I think I have some hot dogs in the fridge."

"Yeah, that'll work. You have ketchup?"

"Pretty sure," Jasper said, walking into the kitchen. "You know, my dad tired to freak me out by telling me about this asteroid that just buzzed the earth. Like, real close call."

"Yeah, my dad told me about that too, strangely enough. Twitter was kind of in a little roar about it, in some corners. But I saw on Yahoo news that the thing was small enough that even if it came the earth's atmosphere would have just disintegrated it anyways."

"Would have made a cool looking falling star," Jasper suggested, looking at the hot dogs plump in the microwave.

"Yeah. I remember seeing a falling star as a kid; a particularly huge one, for some reason. Like, took up all the sky, it seemed like. I was afraid it was a comet that would destroy the earth."

Jasper stood in the kitchen doorway looking at her. "I have a similar childhood memory," he said, baffled by the coincidence.

"It's kind of sad, thinking about it in retrospect. That we saw something that should be thought of as so beautiful, you know. And instead of being in awe we were afraid for our lives."

"Yeah," Jasper said, perplexed that she had guessed right concerning his reaction to the blaze in the sky. "That's so true. Like, I remember a story Stephen Spielberg tells of his dad taking him to a meteor shower as a kid. And he grew up in the desert, in Arizona, you know, back in the 50's or whatever, so the skies were just..."

"Crystal clear," Janelle said, finishing Jasper's sentence.

"Yeah. And he says it inspired him, fired his imagination. And all these years later, he's what, seventy something now or whatever, and he's still got that unlimited boyish imagination which he can tap into, to become... who he was. Or is."

"Right," Janelle said. "I love his movies. I'm a bit of a movie buff."

"I've guessed so," Jasper said. "Did you say in the car that you've seen all of Emma Robert's indie movies?"

Janelle giggled. "Well not all of them. Did you say you wanted her to bump into you? Like, literally?"

Jasper blushed. The Microwave timer chimed. Jasper rolled from the doorway back into the kitchen. Janelle followed him. She opened the fridge and got out the ketchup. "Thank god it's not empty. My dad always puts empty ketchup bottles back in the fridge."

Jasper giggled. "My dad too."

As they ate they talked about Emma Roberts some more, reminiscing about her dumb Nickelodeon kid's shows, humorously sarcastically exaggerating the significance of her kids movies "Nancy Drew" and "Hotel for Dogs," debating whether she got a foot in the door in Hollywood because of her famous aunt or on her own merits. Janelle got Jasper to admit that Selena Gomez has nice boobs.

"Want to watch TV?" Jasper asked.

"Or have sex?" Janelle teased.

They laughed, walking to the couch.

"Where's your dad anyways?" Janelle asked.

"Meeting," Jasper answered. "He's always gone at meetings."

"Mine too," Janelle said.

She's so gorgeous, Jasper thought. He liked to wander the new towns he moved to, the malls, outdoor shopping plazas, school campuses, streets, rails. Scan for pretty girls. Not in a perverse way, he believed (if her were older and uglier, maybe, yeah). Manhattan was a good people watching place; all the modeling agencies there. A lot of skin, but a lot of fat, in the South, but some good stuff. Salt Lake kids dressed surprisingly well. A lot of youth here because of the big Mormon and Catholic families. Repopulate the earth, being a commandment. A lot of bankruptcies in Utah, competing with the neighbors, wanting to keep up appearances, the new Republican thing (was it new?) of worshiping money and those that make a lot of money, and equating this 'success' with Christianity. A girl yesterday wore red rimmed glasses and a red short skirt, had amazing legs and a blond pony tail pulled tightly back; glad I saw her, Jasper thought, remembering the mental image.

But with Janelle, not only did he love simply looking at her, then imagining touching her, but she's the first and only girl he ever saw who he imagined spending the rest of his life with. From the moment he first saw her, in the principal's office. He wanted to cling to her beauty like a baby suckles milk (that metaphor had come to him and then made him wince). There was no beauty before her; she is the god of beauty, the alpha and omega, the beginning and the end. What would our children look like, he wondered. They'd be adorable.

She's just a new girl, I'm just a new boy, he thought, we're just emerging friends, a budding slow burning casual relationship, tied by music, conversation, shared interests. This dumb play.

He flipped through channels and settled on an old G.I. Joe cartoon, some 80's thing, found on some nostalgia cartoon channel. He wondered since her dad was in the military (so she claimed) if she might like this. "This okay?" he asked.

"Heck yeah, of course," Janelle exclaimed. "My older brother used to make me watch these."

"He made you?"

"Well, I ended up liking them. Lady Jay and the Baroness are so bad ass. Too bad the recent live action movies sucked so bad."

Jasper took another bite of his hotdog.

"He moved away, like, what, six years ago? My older brother. Tired of all the moving. And... other things."

"Is he...?"

"He's all right. He's in some punk band in Boston now. So funny, look how big the boobs are on these cartoon girls. Horny dude animators. I don't think they'd get away with that today."

"Yeah, they don't make cartoons like they used to," Jasper said. He thought of her long silky hair and her boobs tight under her light red T-shirt. He didn't want to be a creep or a pervert. He wanted to be respectful. But it couldn't be helped, she made him horny.

"Oh no, I spilled ketchup on my shirt," Janelle exclaimed.

She invited Jasper to look at her chest, where the ketchup had spilled, which he tried not to seem as eager and glad as he really was to be doing. The earlier peeks were quick embarrassing slide glances and peripheral vision stuff, now he could, more or less, full on stare. For a moment. Just to see where the ketchup had spilled.

"Do you have a shirt I can change into? It's kind of a pet peeve of mine to wear dirty clothes."

"Um... sure, yeah." Jasper wondered if she had spilled the ketchup on purpose. His heart beat heavier, imagining the fantasy of her changing her shirt in front of him, her bare torso, her bra, her cleavage, all the soft slopes and wonders, all exposed. He really didn't know her, he realized, despite possibly being in love with her. Was she... *bad?* No, that's not the word. *Daring? Bold? Slutty?* No, that's not the word either. She sort of seemed shy, same as he was, but also sort of not; shy people don't try out for school plays, or, they do, they can, but not the clinically troubled sheltered shy type... right? He remembered what she said to him recently (everything with her was recent, of course, which made it all better) a line which made him fall in love with her more: *I want to be lead by love. Fear too often controls me.* He had wanted to kiss her right after she said it, sitting next to her in the theater chairs looking up at an empty stage. Instead of kissing her he had gulped and said "me too."

He went to his room and opened his T-shirt drawer. He wondered if he were slimy enough to try and pull a trick, like pick the smallest, tightest t-shirt he owned. She was tall-ish, for a girl, around 5-9 or 5-10 he guessed, but all his t-shirts would still look baggy on her. He pulled out something random; it turned out to be a Patriots Superbowl commemorative T-shirt, a nice one, white with blue trim around the arms and collar. He approached her and threw the crumpled up shirt at her. She leaped to catch it, briefly exposing her tight midriff. She stood and locked her green eyes on his, smiling. She took a few slinky steps back, keeping her sly sexy smile, while letting the shirt fall. She snapped it like laundry before folding. Her smile brightened, showing teeth, before she turned around and then said "close your eyes."

Of course he couldn't keep his eyes closed. He didn't believe she really wanted him to anyways. She slipped off her shirt, exposing her back to him, reaching over her neck to sweep her long hair in front of her; her shoulder blades, her petite shoulders, the line marking her spine, the outward curves of her hips, all soft, firm and bare, all naked except for the thin pink bra strap. His heart pounded and he flushed, felt sweat rise up; he felt dazed, having to consciously tell himself he wasn't dreaming. Her back matched that of the girl in his recurring dream. She was the same girl. Except for one big difference. A small tattoo on her upper right shoulder. She slipped on his shirt then slowly spun around while tugging the bottom. She bit her lip, flickered her eyes down then up and blushed, smiling with a mix of embarrassment and thrill, tickled and pleased by Jasper's astonished to stone clumsy stance and expression.

"What was that?" he asked in astonishment.

She shrugged and raised her eyebrows.

"Was that a tattoo?"

"Yeah, just a little thing, no biggie. I actually got it a long time ago."

"Really? So... wait... when?"

"My dad also pierced my ears when I was a baby so..."

"Your dad... put a tattoo on you?"

Janelle chuckled nervously. "I know, kind of crazy right?"

"Is he..."

"He's not like a crazy hippy or anything. He appears quite conservative actually, and I guess he is... in his own mind. I mean, he's normal enough, I guess, no one could tell..."

"Tell?"

"Let's get back to the TV, can we? We're missing G.I. Joe; I think I remember this episode. Cobra just about wins in this one. Evil terrorists."

"Can I... see it? Again? Close up?" Jasper asked nervously, shaken, shaking, yet bold.

Janelle smiled and scrunched her nose. "Well I don't know," she said teasingly, flirty. "I don't think we've even gone on a date yet have we? I thought you told me you were shy?"

"I thought you told me the same thing?"

Janelle shrugged. "You have to show me something of yours first."

Jasper gulped. Yes, he loved this flirty game, but, something else, something possibly even more important, took precedence. He wanted to see her tattoo again not for solely titillating reasons, but to confirm a completely unsexy suspicion. He stood stiffly. He gave her a strange look. One that Janelle had trouble deciphering: scorn, judgment? Definitely not a sexy look. Or if that was the attempt, it was a disappointing failure (as cute as he still looked; annoyingly [or blessedly] one of those guys, Janelle mused, who couldn't look bad even if they tried).

Janelle shrugged, undoing her 'sexy' posture. "Look, did I do something wrong?"

Jasper sighed. "Sorry, I didn't mean to ruin... or irritate you. But... it might be kind of important to me... in a weird way..."

"It's important for you to see my tattoo?" Janelle asked with a hint of irritation.

Normally Jasper would back off; he knew he should back off; that's what she was signaling him to do. But he had to know. He felt an out of body sensation, similar to when he saw the crazy old lady talk about the girl prophet on the YouTube video. Shaken and stunned; unsure of what's real. His curiosity, his desire to confirm what he already knew he saw, overwhelmed his sense of manors or desire not to upset Janelle. Even to risk whatever romantic relationship may develop.

"Yes," he answered.

Janelle looked at him with a steely gaze for a moment. Then she shrugged, gave a little smile and raised her eyebrows. "Okay. If it's that important to you." She tugged down her shirt then lifted it off, this time not going through the pretense of modesty by turning her back to him. Her boobs, the deep cleavage, held comfy and firm in her pink lacy bra, were like a glorious bright flashing light; how their softness, just by their softness, illuminated a glow; how light bounces off skin so much more pleasingly than it does cloth. There she is, standing, nearly all uncovered. The tips of her fingers lightly massaged her collar bone. He imagined her to be smiling pleasingly and flirty again as she had done before; he couldn't raise his gaze up from her cleavage to know for sure. He gulped hard then heard her giggle. He wondered if she were a virgin like himself. He wondered, hoped, if he'd lose his virginity to her soon. Before the end of the world. He told himself to focus. He cleared his throat.

"It's on my back shoulder, here," she said and spun around and brushed her hair in front of her. He stepped near her, then nearer, till all that was in his focus was the tattoo. She giggled.

"I don't really like it," she said. "I'll probably have it removed."

A long seeming and uncomfortable silence followed. "Is everything all right back there stud?" she asked while smiling. He didn't answer. She felt his breath on her back which felt cool and she shrieked and laughed and spun around from the surprise tickle, then made another little shriek from finding herself so close to him, nearly nose to nose, then blushed at the embarrassing realization that her breast may have brushed up against his arm as she spun around; he may have been reaching to touch her tattoo. She put her hands on her cheeks as an impulse to cover her blushing and Jasper noticed as she did so her breasts squeezed closer together, causing rounder deeper cleavage, and then he blushed feeling heat rise in his cheeks. They both took a step back.

"Would you like to see it again?" she asked breathily.

"No," Jasper whispered. He had two fingers pressed against his lips and a look of astonished questioning in his eyes; again, not a "sexy" look, but one she still found alluring, partly due to being confounded herself over what he was thinking.

She chuckled. "It's only a tattoo," she said.

He bit his lip and shook his head. "It's not."

She slipped the shirt Jasper had given her back on.

"It's a red inked M," Jasper said.

"Look, Jasper..."

"Are you prepared to be freaked out?" he asked.

"Um... sure?" she said.

Jasper took off his shirt. He was chiseled. Janelle couldn't help but to smile in satisfaction. Her smile dropped, as did her jaw, when Jasper turned around to expose his back to her and she saw on his right shoulder a small blue tattooed M.

CHAPTER TEN

Cassandra sat with her back against a brick gang graffiti tagged wall in the alleyway between an empty building and a sandwich shop, hugging her knees. The chill dug through her skin, gnawing and chilling her bones, making her numb. She clenched her body. She looked at the white puffs of her breath. She sensed a blizzard coming. A man and a lady emerged in the alleyway and stood as dark silhouettes before approaching. She lifted her eyes to them and they stopped.

The man looked into her eyes. He thought he saw a storm brewing in her pupils. His hopes rose.

"Are you she?" he asked. His body shook.

"Who?" Cassandra asked.

"The girl prophet."

"Should I destroy the world or save it?"

The man gasped. His heart seemed to stop while also beating fast.

"So you are the one! The one who will save us all? Save humanity?"

"So you are from the Blue Mangenie family," Cassandra said.

"I am," Jasper's father answered.

Cassandra stood. "Maybe it would be better if the others catch me. It will take the decision away from me. The burden is so great."

Jasper's father stood perplexed. Decision? He didn't know what she spoke of. The prophecies said she would save the earth, unless she died before the hour of destruction came.

"The others come," Cassandra stated dispassionately.

Another man and women came around the corner and entered the alleyway; they had been jogging and stopped abruptly, surprised to see the alleyway already full of two adults and a little girl, even if it had been what they were expecting. The man was Janelle's father and the woman a top psychic of the cult he led. The two men pulled guns on each other near simultaneously. Cassandra saw the light man and the shadow man come, the light man stood by the leader of the Blue

Mangenie family, the shadow man stood by the Red Mangenie family leader. Cassandra saw that the two psychics from the two cults saw the light and shadow men and were frightened by them.

Janelle's father shot Jasper's father. The lady with Jasper's father shrieked and jumped back. The gun then pointed at her.

"Don't," Cassandra said. "I'll go with you."

She walked towards the man and he pointed his still smoking gun down at her. He grit his teeth.

"No, not now" the lady by him said. "It must be done the right way."

**

Cassandra, her back chained against a stone wall in the basement of the Red Mangenie leader's home (Janelle's home) didn't whimper. Two long white candles flickered on both sides of her.

One by one figures in red hooded silk robes entered the basement room. They had been previously instructed to remain solemn and not make spectacles of themselves once in sight of the girl prophet, the demon child, the key, sign, and symbol of the final destruction, the nature preventer, the one who must be destroyed, Cassandra. They hummed chants in order to keep from gasping or screaming at the sight of her; this girl, the reason for their purpose, the heart of their cult. Generations, centuries of prophecies, now manifest.

The leader entered the room. Janelle came and stood in the back, dressed in a robe, her hood up; the first time she had worn a robe in six years. She didn't kneel like the others or participate in the chants. None thought much of her non-conformity; as the leader's daughter she was granted leniency, similar to how princesses of kings are.

An old lady, one top psychic, approached Cassandra while holding a golden knife. She plunged the tip of the knife into Cassandra's palm and blood trickled out and fell into a silver pan and the center of the pan burst into flames as if Cassandra's blood had been cooking alcohol dropped into a sizzling frying pan. The lady screeched from the pain of the heat yet clutched the pan and held it up for the small congregation to see. Their chants broke apart into gasps and moans. Janelle looked into the pan and saw the image of the earth engulfed in fire followed by scenes of metropolitan cities crumbling from earthquakes and lava spewing up from the earth, as if the cites had been built over active volcanic cauldrons now violently erupting. A shadow raced around the walls of the room loudly cackling. The old lady threw the pan onto the ground and it disintegrated into smoke, leaving a black smear.

This is insane Janelle thought.

"Kill her now!" one of the congregants yelled out, which followed with shouts and murmurings of agreements.

"No!" the leader, Janelle's father said. "It must be done on the full moon. In the right way. In a few days. Otherwise there is no guarantee she will die."

Janelle slipped out the back door and then went up the stairs to the living room then up the stairs to her room, trying to put what she had just seen out of her mind. An impossible task. How strange; all that crazy stuff happening below her while above things could be perceived as the normal dull of ordinary life; Hallmark Christmas specials on the TV, people out shopping, sleeping, taking dogs on walks, baking chocolate chip cookies.

She entered her room, threw off her robe and shut it behind her closet door (she wanted to burn it; like a criminal destroying evidence) and flopped on her bed then looked up at the ceiling. She thought of trying to distract herself with the online world: Facebook, Twitter, celebrity gossip sites. Maybe listening to music would work to distract her; pretend what was happening below, what was below, wasn't real. But she couldn't move. Too tired and heavy; the reality settling over her. The strange, brutal, ghastly reality. *There's a skinny pretty little girl chained to a stone wall in my house and she might be murdered.* The realization struck like a brick through a window. She winced. *But they won't murder her yet; they'll wait till the full moon at least; just forget you saw anything.*

She opened her laptop and updated her Facebook status as "a little freaked out." A little while later a friend from Arizona asked why and she typed back a lie: she had just seen two spiders mating in the sink. She watched some cute cat videos on YouTube. She watched, for the first time, the video that had gone semi-viral, approaching just a million views, of some old lady screeching about the end of the world and a demon girl and a house on fire and a dead father and the end times are nigh and then she mentions *The Mangenie Family*. Janelle quickly shut her laptop, spooked. She thought better of checking the news: it'd just be filled with the usual depressing crime and wars and hatreds and pandering political egotists stoking anger, using so much hyperbole, over how government money is spent, and there's probably more mass shootings, and so on: just depressing stuff. Crazy stuff; how'd we get so crazy, she wondered. Propaganda working its wonders. The allure and appeal of hate; feeling there's injustice done, separating people into groups and *they* are taking what's *mine.* Lack of empathy, lack of reason, special interests and the influence of the oligarchs; it doesn't suit them financially to have people worried over global warming, so they've managed to convince sizable numbers that global warming is a hoax. So that their flow of oil money won't be threatened. So they can buy the third golden toilet bowl in their Aspen home. And so on. Janelle's thoughts unspooling; how'd I get stuck on the disgusting thoughts of politics and crap? Without even checking the news, refusing to check the news; hurricanes, fires, blizzards, droughts.

She got up to shower, to wash away her itchy discomfort; bored but not wanting to do anything, feeling too heavy to do anything like read or listen to music or watch TV. In the shower it struck her again, like a ringing silver bell: *they plan to kill her.*

But they don't see her as a little girl. They see that as just a disguise. They see her as... an evil entity. Because... why... I've tried to forget the teachings... because she wants to pervert nature? She's against natural selection, or human evolution or development... a forest is replenished healthier in time after a fire... that's one of our cult's sayings I believe. Because... she wants to save the earth, save people? And they want it to be destroyed? Anyways, that's all craziness, she's just a little girl, not whoever they think she is. How did it come to this point? How could such normal, happy even, good even, seeming people, including my father... do this? Think these crazy things? Thing such an act as murdering a little girl could be justifiable in any way?

She thought of Jasper. He really was handsome. And cute. Can someone be handsome and cute? More handsome than cute; cute is for puppy love, boy bands and crap. He was strong looking. She thought of romantic comedies and the "bad boy" allure, a farce really, and sex and motherhood. The future. Jasper would make a good father, she could tell. Maybe not the most thrilling of boyfriends, too nice, doesn't seem like the type to take big dumb daring romantic risks and steal for you, kill for you, hurt you to make you obsess over him more because secretly you hate yourself, or whatever the reasons are why so many find hot abusive type boys so thrilling and sexy. He's insular a bit, shy, and shy is cute sometimes but not thrilling, not really what a girl wants in a boy; swagger works, confidence and swagger, even some arrogance; we girls say we hate it yet that's what we so often end up being attracted to, in spurts and bursts anyways, against our better instincts sometimes. But he'd make a great father, as well as lover, and in the end, that's what you really want. Chaos can't be sustained; strength and stability are better paths to long term happiness.

She found herself getting a little bit turned on thinking about Jasper, naked in the shower, which she felt some guilt over; maybe trying to work up arousal was just another way to try and escape the disgusting unthinkable reality of what lay in the basement, a small frail body chained to a wall. She got out of the shower and put on a bathrobe.

They had matching tattoos, same M different colors. Strange, after the realization how they just basically ignored the significance. Didn't speak what they both knew the tattoos signified. They belonged to the two opposing warring cults. After he had shown her his tattoo her heart had hammered. He had put his shirt back on. And she honestly can't say what they next spoke of. Small talk. "Oh, that's neat." "Huh, what are the coincidences?" "What do you think about the Kanye West, Taylor Swift thing? An unlikely celebrity beef, right?"

She texted Jasper. "What are you doing?"

He texted back. "Not much. Memorizing lines. You?"

"Same," she texted back.

"It really is awful."

"lol, I know!" she texted back, although she hadn't really *laughed out loud.*

They switched to chat mode on their phones and she talked with him awhile longer. Mostly over how bad the play was, how no one would ever say some of these lines in any type of reality anyways, especially when Doug the playwright made efforts to try and sound 'poetic' or 'profound' like he were trying to be Shakespeare or something. Although, Jasper mentioned, not like any ever talked or talks like Shakespeare's plays in any type of reality either. And movies aren't reality based either; robots transforming into cars and superhero's and Ninja Turtles and rom-com clichés and junk. And not even reality TV, so called, depicts reality, like those Bachelorette shows; in what real world setting does some dude simultaneously date thirty other women and whisk them off to exotic dates around the world while TV cameras follow? But of course, this all makes sense; people want escape in their entertainment, not to be reminded of the dull routines and disappointments of their real lives. During their talk they both thought, without mentioning, the possibility of similarities between their own situation and Romeo and Juliet; two young lovers (they weren't 'lovers' but both wanted to be) from two warring families, brought together by fate. (Or so they foolishly think). Jasper told her he was worried about his father; he hadn't heard for him in about a day, and although it wasn't uncommon for his father to jaunt off on "business" he usually at least would leave a message. But as soon as he brought it up he realized he didn't want to talk about his father with her; it'd drive the conversation towards cult stuff, which he surmised neither he nor Janelle were ready to discuss yet. Their conversation ended.

Janelle lay in bed, still unable to sleep. Her guilt was torturing her. Here she was, phone flirting with Jasper while a little girl was chained to a wall in her own home. *I'm a monster.* How did slave owner wives deal with the ugly reality? Dismissing it, excusing it, justifying it. They're not humans. They deserve it. God intended it to be this way.

Yet she feared going down to the basement. The clock read 2:00 am. She got up and stood in her room. She heard wind rustle leaves outside. She shuffled over to her door and opened it. She walked down the stairs, feeling out of body, like a ghost. She opened the door to the basement. She felt like throwing up. She felt like she was in a horror movie, the part where the audience screams at the screen to the dumb teen, *don't go down the basement!* The doorknob felt cold; her hand still on it. The door had creaked; she hadn't noticed at first, the creak sound remerging in her mind like an echo. She took a heavy breath and took the first step down the stairs.

The basement room was dark except for two glowing orbs. She realized the two orbs were the little girl's eyes. That can't be right, she thought. She blinked and when she opened her eyes the glowing orbs were gone but a flickering candle light illuminated the little girls face, still chained to the wall. She slowly walked towards the girl. The little girl was pretty. Too gaunt, tragically so, but pretty.

"Did... it hurt?" Janelle asked tepidly, quietly, in a shaky voice.

"No." The girl's voice was soft yet firm.

"Are you scared?"

"No."

"Why?"

"Because I knew it would happen."

"Are you... um... who do you claim to be?" Janelle asked. "I mean, you're just a girl, right? Just a little girl?"

Cassandra didn't answer.

"My dad says...um...it's kind of stupid but... my dad thinks..."

"He's right," Cassandra said.

"Um..." Janelle said then guffawed. "You... um..."

"It's within my power," Cassandra said.

"Um... what is?" Janelle asked.

"The comet. My comet."

"Your..." Janelle uttered then guffawed again.

"Do you sometimes want to throw your life away and start all over?" Cassandra asked.

"Well... I'm a little too young to have thoughts like those."

"You can't lie to me," Cassandra said. "I know you have."

"Well... you know how teens can be... melodramatic sometimes... I mean, of course you don't know, you're... how old are you anyways?"

"Do you think humanity should just be scratched out and start over."

Janelle paused. "What are you asking? Do you mean like... killing people? No, no of course not, are you crazy?"

"Am I?" Cassandra asked.

"What? Yes, I mean, no, no, I don't know, but if you want to kill people? That's crazy."

Cassandra closed her eyes. Her lip quivered and she began to cry.

"Oh no, oh my god, I'm sorry, I didn't mean, I mean," Janelle stammered. She couldn't quite believe where she was, who she was talking to, what she was saying, what she had said. It all felt surreal. "Why are you crying?" Janelle asked tenderly.

"I've seen..." Cassandra said, a whimper through heavy heaves. "So much hate." She then bit her trembling lip again.

"My dad says you'll... destroy the world by trying to save it. Is that true?" Janelle blurted out the question, and then with the words having been said out loud and hanging, felt absurd for saying them.

"What does the father of your friend Jasper say?" Cassandra asked.

"Well..." Janelle said, taken aback. "We haven't really talked... about any of that."

"But you know," Cassandra said.

"Well... he'd say you need to be saved... to save the world. I think."

Cassandra didn't say anything. She didn't mention how Janelle's father had killed Jasper's father and hid the body, wrapped in cellophane, under the floorboards of the basement.

"You say you... control a comet?" Janelle asked. "Is it near?"

"Yes," Cassandra answered.

"Well, why, or I mean, then how come... scientists, NASA, haven't identified it, or seen it, or warned us or something. It's heading for earth I assume?"

"Because it's my comet," Cassandra said.

"Will it hit the earth? Can you make it hit the earth? Or make it miss?"

Cassandra nodded her head.

Janelle stood, unsure. She took a step back and rubbed her eyes and forehead. The room spun. The surreal feeling thickened; was any of this real? Would her dad kill her if she tried to save this girl? Her whole life would take another trajectory. A harder one. She'd have to run away. If he was willing to kill a little girl he'd be willing to do anything. This was a bitter truth, hard to swallow.

"Don't call the police," Cassandra said.

She can read minds, Janelle thought. "Why not?"

"Just don't."

"I have to recue you. I can't... I couldn't live with myself knowing... I'm sorry." She wasn't sure who her *sorry* was addressed to; maybe her father, maybe herself, maybe the world. "Is there a key around here or something, or...?"

"And then what?" Cassandra asked.

"I don't know. Take you back to wherever you came from; where did you come from anyways?" She sighed and covered her face with her palm. "Maybe we'll go to Wendy's and I'll buy you a Frosty. How does that sound?" *Did I just try making a joke or something? Sure, that makes sense, humor diffuses tense situations. Although, maybe I wasn't joking, maybe that's literal, sure, why not? Is Wendy's open twenty four hours a day?*

"Call your boyfriend."

"I'm sorry, who?" Janelle responded.

"Jasper. You'll call Jasper and you two will free me and then drive me to the desert," Cassandra commanded.

"Um... okay?" Janelle said.

Cassandra's eyes seemingly began to glow. "The stars fall from the sky, the night will go black, then there will only be the burning purifying; the destruction to do away with all, then from the ashes of many will arise two who are pure who will start fresh."

Janelle stood stunned, frightened, musing over the apparent nonsense the little girl just spoke so authoritatively; gibberish which should simply be discarded as insane ramblings by some homeless drunk street bum self professed doomsday prophet. The same type of ranting she would roll her eyes at and dismiss when coming from the cult self professed psychics. But these strange words coming from this little girl jolted Janelle, causing her to wonder for a moment if all the rantings of her father may have harbored some truth; that the means through which the world might be obliterated would come in the form of this little girl.

"I...um...what?" Janelle stammered. She thought how if any of her school friends were with her at the moment, if she had any school friends, normal girls from normal families whose fathers didn't drag them all over the country, leading some crazy cult of people bound by eccentric beliefs and rituals, that they would just laugh at this little girls crazy talk (or would they). But Janelle couldn't laugh; she didn't find any humor in it.

"From the ice which falls from the sky will come fire," Cassandra said.

"They've... brainwashed you... somehow," Janelle said. She looked at Cassandra's palm. She could see the mark of the knives slash on it, already beginning to scab. They hadn't even bothered to bandage it. "You know... you realize, they're going to kill you. In four days, during the full moon." Janelle could hardly believe what she just said. The truth and insanity of it. She looked at Cassandra. Cassandra just stared back.

"Does that... scare you?" Janelle asked.

"No," Cassandra answered.

"Why not?" Janelle asked.

"What will be will be," Cassandra answered. "If they succeed in killing me I'll no longer be burdened with my choice."

"Your choice? Concerning what?"

"You," Cassandra said.

"Me?"

"And everyone else," Cassandra said.

Janelle took another step back. A flash of the image of the earth burning, the image she had seen in the silver pan, came to her, not as memory but as a moment. She nearly stumbled over, losing her balance, temporarily blinded by the sudden image which had the effect of a hit between her eyes. She looked into Cassandra's eyes. They frightened her. They appeared to be glowing again, flames inside them. She took another stumbling step backwards. She left the room and ran up the stairs in the dark, falling, getting back up hurriedly. She ran to her room and shut the door; in her safe haven. She texted Jasper. "Are you asleep?"

He answered back almost immediately. "No. Woke up by a dream/nightmare right before you texted."

Janelle was afraid to ask what he dreamed of.

"The girl is here," she typed into her phone, heaved a breath then hit send.

CHAPTER ELEVEN

Jasper came over right away. 3:00 am. They went into the basement together. Light and shadow seemed to be swirling, dancing around each other, around the walls. "Stop it," Cassandra said and the light and shadow stopped and the candle by her face lit up.

"Oh my god," Jasper said.

"Or something like that," Janelle responded.

Jasper looked at her. He recognized her from the paintings and drawings the psychics had done; or from his dreams; maybe both.

"You can come closer," Cassandra instructed.

Janelle and Jasper approached closer.

"What's your name?" Jasper asked in an astonished whisper.

"Cassandra."

Jasper wheezed a throaty laugh then looked at Janelle wide eyed. She shook her head. *Cassandra?* She'd been known by so many names among the cults. But her name is simply Cassandra. The prophesied one has an ordinary name. And she's just a bony little girl.

"How do we save you?" Jasper asked.

The clamps and chains around Cassandra's wrists and ankles glowed and then popped and fell and she was free of them.

"How did you do that?" Jasper asked.

"My friends," she answered. She walked towards the door, passing Jasper and Janelle. Then she turned around and said to them: "you'll take me to the desert now."

"Um... excuse me?" Jasper asked.

"She said the same thing to me," Janelle said.

"Well... why not?" Jasper suggested.

"Really?" Janelle asked.

Jasper shrugged.

"Well, we have school tomorrow."

Jasper laughed lightly at Janelle's joke. She were joking, right? She smiled weakly in response to his laugh.

"But... do we have enough money? Food, gas... and..."

"Come on," Jasper said.

"You both have to come," Cassandra said.

"Um... okay... I guess I'll go pack?" Janelle offered.

"No time," Cassandra instructed.

"You heard her. We'll buy new cloths on the way back or something. I'll buy you an outfit. And clean underwear."

Janelle laughed through a smirk. *Well girls are always saying how they want boys to take them to new places, go on adventures,* she mused.

"Sorry, I blurt out strange things late at night," Jasper said.

"Hurry, before your father wakes up," Cassandra said.

"Well okay," Janelle relented.

The three walked out the front door and into Jasper's car. He turned on the engine. "I don't know where to go," he said.

"I'll show you," Cassandra answered. She guided him to the I-15 North Las Vegas exit.

"I love Las Vegas," Janelle said. "Or, sometimes, when I don't hate it."

Jasper drove for a few hours. The sun had come up. Janelle slept. They stopped in a diner along some little town for lunch and got gas. Jasper had discovered his father's wallet in the car. Cassandra told him the PIN number of his father's debit card. After lunch Janelle drove while Jasper slept. Cassandra didn't sleep. She didn't talk either except to give directions.

"My father hasn't returned," Jasper said when he and Janelle were both awake. "Two days. Two and a half."

"Are you worried?" Janelle asked.

Jasper pressed in his lips. "Like I say, he'll take off sometimes. But he at least leaves a message."

"What about the other members? Have you talked to them?"

Jasper shook his head. "I haven't really had contact with any of them for awhile."

"I know how you feel," Janelle said. "I don't consider those people a part of my family either. But you should call them, maybe they know..."

Jasper picked up his phone.

"Don't," Cassandra said.

When she spoke the phone felt five times heavier in Jasper's hand.

"I'm sorry," Cassandra said. "My father is dead too."

Dead?

Jasper realized he had already known. And he felt oddly calm about it. He didn't know, couldn't explain why. Maybe a 'calm before the storm' type of sensation; maybe later he'd deal with the emotions and ramifications. At the moment he felt... strangely peaceful about it, like someone knowing he will die and has given up the fight is resigned to either feel peace over the coming death or dread and chooses peace, or peaces chooses him; the white light of the afterlife already reaching, calling. Janelle didn't know what to say. She would offer futile attempts at consoling, as one is awkwardly obliged to do at hearing sad news of a friend, yet she sensed he neither wanted nor needed to hear such sorrowful platitudes. You choose to accept fate at some point, and there is peace in acceptance. But he still felt weird, about everything. They drove on in silence. They stopped at a rest stop and switched driving duties again.

"How much further?" Jasper asked.

"Not much further," Cassandra answered. "Until the light fades."

Just as she had said, at sunset, she instructed Jasper to pull to the side of the highway. Then she got out and started to walk into the desert.

"Come," she said.

"What?" Janelle said.

"Where are you going?" Jasper asked.

"Come," Cassandra said again.

"You can't just go walking out in the desert," Janelle said in a low voice to Jasper. "People die that way." She then yelled out to Cassandra: "you can't just go walking out into the desert!"

Cassandra kept walking, her back to them.

"What is she doing?" Janelle asked.

"I don't know," Jasper answered.

Janelle saw in his eyes that he wanted to chase Cassandra, follow her. "I'm hungry Jasper. Let's not follow her."

"We've come all this way. Aren't you curious?" Jasper asked.

"Sometimes you have to just let curiosity go," Janelle answered. She found that she had been holding his arm, tugging on it, close to him.

"We wanted to save her, remember? We can't just..." Jasper's sentence trailed off.

"She's... different. She's not what she seems," Janelle said.

"I'm going," Jasper said. He freed his arm and ran after Cassandra.

"Jasper wait!" Janelle yelled. "Run after her, pick her up, drag her back here. She weighs what, ten pounds?"

"I don't think that would work," Jasper yelled back.

"Jasper wait!" Janelle yelled, then she too ran out into the desert after Cassandra.

The three walked together as the sun went down and the stars emerged, brilliant in the sky.

While walking a lizard crawled over Janelle's shoe. It brought a forgotten memory to her. a flashback. She was a child in the worship room. A cult psychic was giving her a reading, prophesying over her, to her. She told her she'd be instrumental in the decision of the end times. Three signs to look for before you do what you must. And one of the signs was something about a lizard running over her foot. Not said in that way; the words were vague; were strange and rambling and weird, trying to be poetic, in the style whenever the psychics got going and chanted, but there was something about a lizard running over her foot. Which, she recalls, even as a child, she had thought must contain some symbolic meaning beyond her grasp (like most prophecies) rather than anything literal. Yet strange, how that once forgotten memory would pour over her so profusely at this moment. *And a boy in blue who shares the first of your name will walk with you,* the psychic had said; Janelle suddenly recalled it, the voice saying it, as clearly as if the old lady had said it out loud to her at that moment.

Cassandra stopped. A boulder, seemingly randomly dropped among the desolate dry hard flat ground and sagebrush, seemed to suddenly emerge within their sight. Cassandra looked up at the stars. Then she walked towards the boulder.

"How do you feel?" Jasper asked Janelle.

"Very, very strange," Janelle answered.

"Yeah, me too," Jasper said. "Like... sudden déjà vu... for some reason. I can't explain it."

"I feel the same," Janelle said.

Cassandra climbed up on the boulder and stood atop it. She spread her arms out and tilted her head back.

Janelle's heart throbbed. She had been keeping a knife in her back pocket. She took it out and rushed towards the boulder. Then she heard a bang. A gunshot. And she fell. And she realized she had been shot in the back.

Cassandra looked down from the boulder at Janelle. Then she looked at Jasper, holding the gun he had kept in his sweatshirt pocket. He looked up at her, tears in his eyes.

He loved her.

Then he saw a light in the sky illuminating behind Cassandra's head. He at first thought Cassandra's head had started to shine, but no, the light came from beyond her, from the sky. He gasped. He heard a thundering in the sky. Cassandra tipped her head back, her arms outstretched, her eyes closed. Cassandra smiled. Her comet passed over.

End

Janelle's Notebook of Poems

Black lipstick, purple mascara She's rebelling, her name is Sara All she wants for X-Mas is a butterfly Knife to metaphorically slice at life And her skin, brazen, see how deeply She can cut to be cool show off to her Hardcore friends—where did my Daughter go laments her parents Wondering when her dark phase will end

*

To feel deeply love deeply Care deeply otherwise it's all Numb and not as fun—but Caring hurts too—every good Thing requires sacrifices.

*

She said she had a good week, shook hands With real world reality, played in nostalgia And had new adventures, new beginnings, took A picture Of her and her childhood best friend riding Thunder Mountain Railroad And a picture of the silver sparkle fireworks Illuminating Cinderella's castle And sang in the Main Street Christmas parade to Be shown Christmas morning That's just twenty days away, realize it with Exclamation marks and anticipation Wonder what Santa will bring, health, beauty, Prosperity, she said she's climbing levels She's rather artistically poetic sometimes when She wants to be—he tweeted he had a Accomplished Sunday morning, ate some Octopus laughed till his stomach hurt

*

Kiss the bullet wet blood Metal on the mouth the brain Blown tries to heal itself to Speak again—they think they'll Be hero's against the government They love their guns have fantasies They're all crazy, crazy stupid, what Is it about America that encourages The gun-nuts, why do you need Military machine guns in your house How is it a crazy can go buy a Semi-automatic and unload it At an Arizona Safeway and the NRA and Gun-nuts say well that's just the price to pay for Our gun rights The cost (6 dead including a nine year old) is Worth it—my god

*

Kiss me I'm magic A rock slide by accident My name all matches light me wonder What catches and spreads—it's nice to have Dreams, it's nice to want things, thudded the Sarcastic answer unsurprisingly

*

Maybe if you were here maybe I'd miss you When you'd leave, the music is nice fills up The bookstore I'm reading the Q list magazine Best albums of the year—where were you

*

HUNGER GAMES FAN-FIC:

THE BIRTH OF SNOW

Cinna instructed Katniss to spread her arms straight out. He put his finger to his lip and studied her, calculating measurements in his head. "Have you heard the tale of the birth of Snow?" he asked her.

"No," Katniss answered.

"You can put your arms down sweetheart."

Katniss obeyed him and looked at him questioningly.

"You're prettier than you should be," he said.

"Thank you?" Katniss said, unsure if he had given her a compliment or rebuke.

"Go ahead, sit down," Cinna said with a sigh.

Katniss sat. "Hard to imagine Snow had a mother," she muttered.

Cinna lightly laughed. "Well technically he'd have to, wouldn't he? Although... well... I've said enough."

"What?" Katniss asked.

Cinna sighed. "Well, we all know who his father was. President Frost."

"I've only seen the statues of Frost... and the songs of praise we're made to sing."

"Some say he was worse than Snow," Cinna mumbled through fingers over his lips.

"What?" Katniss asked.

Cinna cleared his throat and glanced at the white walls at the sides before looking back at Katniss. She hadn't taken her eyes off him.

"Yes... there is a beauty hidden under your intensity," Cinna said. "Or a beauty in your intensity. Your eyes... that color... I have never seen anything like them."

"My mother says they are my father's eyes," Katniss said through tight lips. She always felt a hot pang of simmering anger when talking of her father; the injustice of never having really known him.

"Yes... grey... quite fitting the color of smoke... you being from District 12 and all, with the Cole there," Cinna said.

Katniss continued staring at him, unflinching. She sensed that her stare had a force on him which would cause him to crack, to reveal something to her he didn't want to.

"Grey is such a cold color, isn't it?"Cinna said. "But where there is smoke there is fire. There's a fire in you, isn't there Katniss Everdeen," he said, his voice drifting into a whisper.

"Tell me of the birth of Snow," Katniss said.

Cinna chuckled. "It's forbidden. Outlawed. Whoever's caught telling the... what they call filthy myth, is executed."

Katniss kept her intense gaze on him.

"Oh very well," Cinna said, throwing his hands up and rolling his eyes dismissively, probably thinking something along the lines of 'well she'll be dead soon anyways,' Katniss thought.

"Thank You," Katniss said.

"In the history of the games there have only been three times when the games have been nullified and erased from record. You've probably heard that none but Haymitch had ever won from your district."

"Yes," Katniss confirmed.

"Not true," Cinna said mischievously with a raised eyebrow. "Her name was Circa. I'll tell you this quickly," Cinna said, flicking his eyes off the walls, "so forgive the lack of narrative flourishes."

"Please continue," Katniss said.

"She brought a lover with her to the games. A boy named Phillip."

"Quite... improbable that a pair of lovers would be selected at the reaping... the odds are..."

"Here's another little secret daring," Cinna said, interrupting Katniss, raising an eyebrow. "There is no luck in who is chosen. Or, I suppose 'luck' is entirely the wrong word."

"But..." Katniss began.

"The. Government. Controls. Everything," Cinna said, uttering each word as a capitalized self contained sentence for emphasis.

Kantiss finally took her eyes off Cinna, contemplating the shocking possibility. "But... Prim... why would they chose her?"

Cinna shrugged. "She was a pretty girl, wasn't she? Young and innocent. Good for television. Either that or someone wanted her dead."

"But..."

"Dear, I was telling a story, please don't derail me," Cinna said.

"Sorry. Please continue," Katniss said, a bit flummoxed, holding in anger.

"Her name was Circa. Her lover was Phillip. They came from Distrcit 12, your district. They were weak and untrained, but clever. They hid and ran while the others killed each other. No one had targeted them because no one had considered them a threat. Their own method of attack was poison. That and luck. Anyways, long story short, it came down to three, Circa, Phillip and a strapping large warrior boy from district two whose name no one seems to know; pity since he turned out to be quit heroic and noble, unofficially of course; officially he was a traitorous cheater... that is, if the record had been kept."

"What did he do?" Katniss asked.

"He had broken Phillip's limbs, his arms and legs, so Phil laid on his back, helpless, while the district two tribute held the point of a trident to Circa's throat, ready to kill her."

Cinna inhaled deeply and then he put a finger over his lip to try and keep it from quivering.

"Then what happened?" Katniss asked.

"Phillip screamed out 'She's pregnant! She's pregnant'". Cinna paused and closed his eyes. Katniss waited for him to speak again.

"And then... of course the district two boy thought it was a trick. But he paused. He had done so much killing. So much... murdering. He was tired of it and he paused. 'feel my stomach' Circa said to him. And he dropped his trident and kneeled by her side. And he put his hand on her stomach. And he looked into her terrified crying eyes. And he decided that she was telling the truth. And something... clicked in him. He remembered that he was just a boy himself. With his own mother. And he whispered to her, pleading as a boy would to his mother 'what do you want me to do?'

And Circa said to him, whispering, 'I will name him after you. And I will raise him to learn right from wrong. I will make him strong. I will teach him to resist madness."

"What did he do?" Katniss asked, wide eyed.

"He picked up his trident. And he plunged it in Phillip's chest. Then he picked up the sword by Phillip's chest. And while looking straight into the camera he said, 'this madness ends now'. Then he plunged the sword through his own gut."

"Suicide?" Katniss asked.

"Self sacrifice," Cinna answered back, clearly moved by the story. "He could not bring himself to kill a mother. He'd rather die instead."

"So... Circa won."

"Yes," Cinna said flippantly, "she 'wow'. Here's another secret. There is no 'winning' the Hunger Games."

"But..."

"Look at your mentor, Haymitch. Ask yourself, what has he won?"

"His... life," Katniss stammered.

"Ask yourself, in a world such as this, what prize is that?"

"I..." Katniss stammered, shocked, for she never thought she'd hear anyone, especially a Capital citizen, talk in such a way. "No," Katniss said, "you're trying to weaken my resolve..."

"No, my dear, honey, no," Cinna said. "I'm sorry, that was not my intention; I should have kept my mouth shut."

"So... what happened to Circa?" Katniss asked.

"I think you can probably figure that out," Cinna answered.

"But they couldn't have killed her; that's breaking the rules, she won, she..."

"So young, so naïve," Cinna said. "They let her deliver the baby first. They treated her as a winner for about nine months or so. They televised the delivery of her baby. Then right after they executed her live on television. Electrocution. Frost took her baby and raised him as his own. Groomed him to take over the presidency, taught him to rule as ruthlessly, as tyrannically..." Cinna quickly slapped his hand over his mouth, quickly glanced at the walls, then closed his eyes.

"So Crica's baby... became Snow," Katniss said.

Cinna nodded his head yes.

End.

*

#

*

And I wish you were here And I wish I didn't care Blood spilling over the balcony Into the symphony Ghosts groan they can't go home Or write dumb poems or see new songs And hear new movies on the internet I don't want to die I want to dance and feel all right, not holed up Staring at a brick wall And if you hold me tight Maybe we'll get through all right One spin one chance to ignite and be bold Scaling up this brick wall Falling down from life

*

It's a slow pace but it's nice To have a racing heart sometimes, the cement Too hot to walk on so You jump in the sand and race to the waves and It's nice sometimes when it's dark and Raining and I guess I don't feel like going to any Movies; just sit here wondering putting on extra Socks and songs play while in them Sometimes they're great then they're gone and Ended and the feeling is lost

*

Well blaze away, they say Isn't it nice to be strange And wear lighting scars streaked across our Faces Stars like glitter gulping up lighting bugs Kissing baby pet pigs and joining in hugs Fly away to London smear the monarchy Be young, be sweet, be free, melt cheese

*

I've become so bad at it Still, great is great Massage the grape before squeezing the grape Fermented into wine if you partake and can Stand Riding the quake I fall down ashamed during the shake I fall down ashamed, make no mistake Pretty is pretty and ugly is ugly And it's rather easy to differentiate, at first And hunger is hunger and thirst is thirst And the best which is best and worst which is worst Becomes worse Becomes a muddled gray, through age, and Righteous and wrong ways

*

Of course it's not something supposed to be Popular; wouldn't work in mass Well why even bother then, if something can't Be universally loved then it's just crap Well, to do what I want, and maybe it will find Its circle of devotee's, well anyways, then The baby cries and he's snapped back to reality And apologies.

*

Everything fritters away And by the end of the day what you have left is That which you've worked for Mostly in vain Or the relationships made Rotting to decay Or the memories of the play Grasping at the ways they were when felt while In them And on a whim, well here's a new one Work hard to stay sane, play hard to have fun Don't be afraid when it all goes away

*

It's all so exciting, right? The height before the fall, the gown worn to the Ball The crickets at nightfall, the shake the floor The wind swept in from the slam of the door The eerie feeling, have I been here before The making of the clogs and frosting tip of the Cake The job over and done and ready to celebrate Then put it away and wait

*

Funnel cloud moves in The death toll in Joplin rises Since when did he lose the will to win When the sine has been scrubbed off of prizes You're here so be here, sit here, reading opinions and debates Facing dates dreading life, interviews and fate Falling ahead into ages So then also burn all these pages

*

A perfect day may be a photo shoot with puppies She said; then a car hit her and she lay dead Puppies licking her face

*

Well you're out there just slopping Throwing soap bars at sea foam Crushing and crying digging fingernails in wet sand I just don't understand how you get so dramatic Flail like a lunatic over something so small A lack of wants confused as needs A hot sneeze, a nose bleed You'll be okay, really At least I got a quick smile from your craziness around Now just go and be sound

*

Strangling a rock is useless It doesn't break or make water and if you throw it It just plops out in front relatively not very far Away Maybe one day it hurled through space; is Millions, billions, of years old But sits there, just plain, grey and still the same

*

Hold me tight don't hit me Crashing down stumbling thumping in dirt Clawing at walls searching for space To fill hope and something new and who knew And you can't throw yourself back And start over and take back, all those dumb Lines and dumb ideas and wasted dreams and Everything

*

Apathy and teen angst Are standard fodder for indie films They often play out In coming of age movies Where anti-social characters Make sensitive observations seemingly Far beyond their years... The notion of a loner Teenage boy connecting With one of the prettiest Girls at school Is one of those wish-fulfillment fantasies From arrested development Or at least the desire To right the wrongs They experienced as overlooked High-schoolers

*

He said come here sugar it's a wonder How the twilight twirls the stars circular through The night And you twirl your hair smile lips candy coated It's your mind which fascinates me but I'd like To see you in your polka dot bikini lying on the Beach, he said, was it a reach

*

I like the thought of The sun pounding me It takes just a little light To illuminate the world At the microcosmic level Everything, the grass blades Are translucent

*

Ride bike swerving sunny evening the brother Misses your head with the water balloon the White puffy cloud Soon will burn violet pink from the sunset Reaching up grabbing on and lay in bed later Remembering hunting grasshoppers catching Them in jars and the big one that You ran away from Later when much older getting in a car A song comes on reminds you of a childhood Memory and you smile

*

It's best not to fear death Or people, but live, what harm can they do Finding out all about you, hating you, scolding You, you're failing them Then failing yourself then failing god and then They're all connected; best not to think too Much about death What comes next, nothing, or people, if you Want to unfreeze and feel free in life Success or failures, people, lovers, haters Debates for later

*

Scream out wind, be soft Carry me gently but away in violent speeds Feed me I'm hungry, soft white rolls Butter rainbows, it's sickening, barf down on Birds, blow up volcanoes scream at ghosts, go Away, you're gross Let me play, swing high, kick high, drive fast But careful Get by, sunny day to cool night

*

Laugh spasms there's nothing A slight delay in reading lips, synchronize me Heart Say anything bang anything in harmony Be free, lightly tingled air brush up on the side Die inside lovely Every day a treat, love spasms there's nothing There but air, hope, carried away Smile wide in the brew anyways, gulp down Nature city lights candy delights and carnival Frights

*

Beaconing lights Beach scavenging Peaceful scene The flowers and birds Sky, the sun in it, moving across Lazily, slowly; what's the magazine say, What's the numbers And stories of sex, fashion, love, despair, triumph, and celebrities, the world What do you recommend reading

*

A toe tickle A little suck A muck to make of it Mud spit Well that was interesting Wasn't it

*

Don't tell her you love her Till you see me ride my ponies she said Out in the grassy pasture I'll cut all the hairs of my dolls For you, I'll go barefoot through the trail And grow a tail and get skinny, let me have a Chance I'll do a dance Work on it and put it on the screen for you to see Please watch me She said, a bit mad a bit more than crazy, got Him for a moment A house burned down and that was all that was Left Ten years later he sometimes wonders about her When he thinks of other sorry crazy girls Hoping his daughter won't be one; and where is She now

*

It's kind of sad but not really This is over just about I guess why drag death Around, heavy empty body dead Just for something to do; well with it over now What do I do Work on life I guess; well yes, but then, well Failures pile up and up and guess you give up You runt Snuff out fires before they Destroy you, you guilty guy, gal, you what an Embarrassment; guess it's sad it didn't work out More than sad it must end, ugly malformed Unknown hopefully of course it's unknown but Well what was the point of it all or anything or This next one; well, it's not over yet, but I've Given up and that's a strange position to still be In after all this wasted time and money. But we Had some fun times didn't we, try but fail death Darling chocking on our own breaths at this Point last breaths left of rotten inward flesh

*

Keep me whole Pure wheat, insects eat me Skin like honey, sweet to them, disgusting Creatures Don't know they're disgusting, they just go for The taste Waste this place, old motel room A peephole, alone, angels watching to record A sour note of discord A bad thing misused the honey Sucking through the rotten teeth Please love me tell me I can be good anyways Pray for it I guess

*

www.ingramcontent.com/pod-product-compliance
Lightning Source LLC
LaVergne TN
LVHW040949150826
845672LV00002B/598

* 9 7 9 8 2 3 0 4 2 6 7 4 5 *